Mi'ca
Buffalo Hunter

by

Jane Bendix

Illustrated
by the author

Council for Indian Education
517 Rimrock Road
Billings, Montana 59102

To Reinhard

Special thanks to the Editor
Hap Gilliland

Published in Germany as Mi'ca: Büffeljäger
Anrich Verlag

Copyright © 1992 by Jane Bendix

ISBN-0-89992-131-0
SAN-689-836X

The Council for Indian Education is a non-profit organization devoted to teacher training and the publication of materials to aid in Indian Education. All books published by the Council are selected by an Indian editorial board and are approved for use with Indian children. Proceeds are used for the publication of more books for Indian children.

Editorial Board
Hap Gilliland - Chairman
Rosalie BearCrane - Crow
Marie Reyhner - Navajo
Theresa Woodenlegs - Northern Cheyenne
Robert LaFountain - Chippewa
Kay Streeter - Sioux
Annette Reid - Tolowa-Yurok
Elaine Allery - Chippewa-Cree
Sally Old Coyote
Juanita Jackson - Blackfeet
William Spint - Crow
Dolly Plumage - Chippewa-Cree
John J. Woodenlegs - Cheyenne
Jean BearCrane - Crow
Mary Theresa One Bear - Cheyenne
Diane Bakun - Alaska
Jon Reyhner - Indian Ed., EMC
Elizabeth Clark - Secretary of the Board

Contents

1. Doubts 5
2. Making the Bow 16
3. The Arrows 32
4. Moccasins 48
5. Vision-quest 56
6. Tangled Hoof 74
7. The Chase 94
8. The Great Plains 110
9. Lakota Captive 132
10. Sun'kawakan 144
11. Buffalo 162
12. Swift Arrow 180

1
Doubts
1740

All across the Great Plains the new green grass was growing up through the mat of last year's brown tangle. The early spring winds were blowing and the warm sunshine made everything it touched feel vigorous and renewed. A Sioux Indian boy, his long black braids flying in the wind, ran through the grass. Beside him two young dogs leaped and bounded with exuberance. As the boy yelled and the dogs barked, birds cried out in alarm at the noise that shattered the quiet of the Plain. When all three were out of breath they sprawled on the grass and rolled and tumbled with one another.

The boy, Mi'ca (whose full name was actually Mi'caksica, or Coyote) patted the dogs and scratched them behind the ears. He felt troubled. He knew that it was time for him to begin his Vision-quest. He would soon have to prove his manhood and skills by staying alone in the wilderness. Only then would he be asked to join the Men's Society.

To get his mind off the ordeal of the Vision-quest he began to talk to the dogs as though they could understand every word. He explained to them that he was soon going to begin to train them to pull heavy loads, and that whenever the camp moved they would drag poles behind them which would be piled high with the belongings of the tribe. The dogs' tongues hung from their mouths as they panted beside him, but their ears were pricked up and they watched his face as he spoke to them. Mi'ca ran his hands across their chests and under their ribs, explaining how the straps would hold the poles in place. Then he held each dog's jaw together and told them they must also learn not to bark, as that might frighten off game or betray the camp to an enemy.

"But," he said, "I really don't feel like beginning lessons today!" And with that he rolled on his back and the dogs began nuzzling his hands and tugging at his moccasins. When Mi'ca did not respond to them they began chasing one another. Mi'ca just lay there on his back watching the clouds drift by, and dreamed of his upcoming Vision-quest. Like all his friends, he could hardly wait for this most important event of his life, yet he worried. Was he ready? He knew that once he became a warrior and a hunter, he must be always alert, to see every sign of nature that might indicate the presence of an enemy, or of wild game to feed the family. The snap of a branch far off in the forest could tell him someone lay in ambush. A track in the dust, or a broken twig on a bush beside the trail could tell him an elk, or an enemy warrior had passed. He must not miss the sign and he must know which it was.

Yet, Mi'ca was a dreamer. Too often he missed the little things while he dreamed of the big ones to come. He dreamed of the buffalo he would bring home to feed the hungry tribe, but he failed to see the chipmunk that darted under the log. Could he develop all the habits of attention? Could he learn all he needed to know to pass his manhood tests? Would he really have a vision and find a guiding spirit? He pictured a cougar leaping down beside him as he awaited the animal that would be his guiding spirit. He visualized a wolf leading him down the trail. Or, perhaps it would

Coyote
Mi'caksica

Slow Trot   Gallop

Right Front   Right Hind

be the great bald eagle! He gazed again at the sky, where even now his all powerful guiding spirit might appear.

A streak across the blue brought him back to reality as a big grasshopper landed on his leg, folded its wings, and waved its antennae at him. "Not you!" Mi'ca exclaimed, as he roughly brushed the hopper away and felt frustrated with himself for again being off in a world of dreams.

Mi'ca rolled over again and gazed out across the tall grass. It was wonderful to be back on the plains again. All winter his tribe, the Dakota Sioux, had camped in the deep woods much farther to the north and east. The trees had given good protection from the snow and winter storms and he and his friends had been able to play many games on the ice, but the place Mi'ca liked best of all was the open plains. Here he felt free and happy. He wished he could spend the rest of his life on the plains. The thought of racing across the prairie like an antelope or a buffalo excited him. With that thought he jumped up and ran after the dogs. They raced each other across the flat landscape until they had all three exhausted themselves. Finally, Mi'ca turned and called "Weh, weh, weh!" to the dogs and together they ran back towards the camp.

The campsite the tribe had chosen was a grassy meadow at the edge of a large river, already swollen by spring floods. It was a meeting place where different tribes gathered to exchange things of which they had too much for things they needed. Mi'ca's band had been the first to arrive. Mi'ca's mother had set up her tipi near those of his uncle and grandfather so that the family could be close and share in the work. But the rest of the tipis were all around them and everyone was used to sharing everything.

There were a great many dogs in camp, more dogs than people, and as Mi'ca and his dogs returned to the campsite several of the

Squirrel
Zi'ca

camp dogs came out to greet them. The dogs sniffed each other and then all ran off together. Mi'ca looked about the camp. It seemed deserted. The good weather in this month of the Moon-of-the-red-grass-appearing had made everyone want to be out and doing something. Mi'ca went down to the river bank and sat watching the sunlight reflecting off the ripples. He picked up a pebble and skipped it across the surface of the water until it finally dropped and formed rings which spread wider and wider until they were lost in the current.

He fell into a dreamy mood again. When he joined the Men's Society what would his place in the tribe be? Should he become a scout, or a leader of a hunting band? He gave a sigh, he knew that what he really wanted to do more than anything else was to hunt buffalo out on the plains. But his tribe, the Wahpeton Dakota, the Dwellers-among-the-leaves, only rarely came to the Great Plains, and the Buffalo never came into the forest. They ate the prairie grass and ran in great herds, sometimes blackening the whole landscape, or so the scouts had told him. He could almost imagine what that would look like; rolling plains with big shaggy beasts pawing and snorting and thundering along as far as the eye could see.

The smallest reflection of a shadow fell across the water in front of him, and Mi'ca held very still. He had been startled, but he had not jumped. One could not hope to catch game in the wild if one's own actions were not as quiet as those of the animals who lived in the forest. Without making a sound Tato'ka, Mi'ca's uncle, had come up behind him. Mi'ca slowly turned his head to look up at him.

"Hou!" he said.

"Hou!" said Tato'ka.

Chipmunk
Hetkala

Mi'ca was very fond of Tato'ka. His eyes were always so sparkling and seemed ready to crinkle with laughter. But they were also very keen eyes which didn't miss the slightest movement of the birds and animals around him. Tato'ka was one of the best bowmen of the tribe.

Each day before the sun rose above the horizon the hunters started out on the trail. The boys of the camp made a game of who would spot the first hunter to return. They would be deeply engrossed in some sport, but would keep watch out of the corners of their eyes. The watching got more intense as the day wore on. Mi'ca was especially proud if he could shout, "Hu-hu-hu!" at the top of his voice when his Uncle was the first to return with a large deer on his shoulders. Mi'ca smiled up at this uncle at the thought.

Tato'ka smiled back and put his hand on Mi'ca's shoulder and said, "You are growing tall and strong. It is time for you to learn to take your place among the men of the Wahpeton. I will teach you what I have learned of the ways of the animals which are about us. Now, can you tell me what animals have come to this spot to drink?

Mi'ca knew Tato'ka expected him to be alert to every sight and sound of nature, but he had again been so distracted by his thoughts that he had failed to notice the tracks on the river bank. One quick glance and he answered, "Squirrels and chipmunks."

"Yes, good!" said Tato'ka. "But how do you tell them apart?"

Mi'ca squatted beside Tato'ka and pointed at a set of tracks. "The squirrel tracks are larger and the pattern they make shows that they climb trees because the front paws come down at the same time and then the hind paws do also. The chipmunk runs with his front paws coming down one behind the other and only the back paws come down at the same time."

Tatoka smiled and nodded his head, then stood up and began to walk back towards the woods. Mi'ca tried to rise up as quietly as Tato'ka had and to hold himself as straight and tall as he could. Tatoka pointed to an oak tree where a squirrel had flattened himself out on a high branch. When the squirrel saw that he had been spotted, he raised himself up and began scolding and chirping with little staccato noises.

The little striped chipmunk was harder to find, but eventually they saw one sitting up on his haunches for a moment before he scampered behind a rock pile. He, too, began to scold, calling "Chock-chock," and then "Chock, chock, chock!" and keeping up the chatter until the two walked away.

"You know the saying, 'Aki-ta mani yo,' - observe everything around you as you walk. A scout must do that if he wants to become a good tracker. You must also train your nose to recognize the scents of animals. One small chipmunk does not leave much of a scent to be recognized, but a whole burrow will have a recognizable scent. A trail of footprints will never be perfect and may be lost altogether if the animal runs across rocks. Then other signs will become important; a tuft of hair caught on a bush, or a pile of seed husks where the animal stopped in the sunshine to eat some of the seeds stored in its cheeks,' said Tato'ka.

Tato'ka stood tall and straight and looked directly into Mi'ca's eyes and then said, "I will come to you every day now, until it will be time for your Vision-quest. You are observant and able to shoot small game and birds with your small bow and blunt arrows. But now it is time for you to have a man's bow and to hunt larger animals to help feed our camp, and perhaps to become a warrior to protect our people from our enemies."

Mi'ca had never heard his uncle speak to him so seriously, and although he wanted to jump up and hug his uncle at this news, he knew that from now on he would have to treat his uncle with reserve and respect instead of with whoops and hugs. Tato'ka was speaking again. "Now you must go to grandfather, Tun'kan'si'dan, who will also help to prepare you for your Vision-quest."

Mi'ca nodded his head and was deep in thought for a moment. When he turned to speak to Tato'ka, Tato'ka was gone, as quietly as he had come.

Flaking a tool

Decorated Tipi Lining
Wanhi kagapi

2
Making the Bow

When Mi'ca reached the campsite he found his grandfather sitting cross-legged chipping an arrowhead. This had always seemed a tedious job to Mi'ca, but when he thought of having his own arrows he looked at his grandfather's work with more interest. When Grandfather finally stopped he looked up at Mi'ca and said, "Bring me your bow and arrows, Mi'ca, and let me see how well you can shoot."

Mi'ca ran to get them and on his way back saw a group of his friends running races. They yelled to him to come join them, but he only waved his bow at them and shook his head. Grandfather had seemed as serious as his uncle, and now running even one short race with his friends didn't seem to be the right thing to do.

When he reached his grandfather he strung his bow and held it in his left hand. Grandfather looked up and pointed to a knot in a tree trunk not far away. Mi'ca placed the arrow notch on the string and raised the first finger of his left hand, which held the bow to let the arrow rest on his knuckle. Then he slowly pulled the string back to his cheek as he took aim. It was an easy shot and Mi'ca gave a sigh of relief when it hit the target exactly.

"Now," said Grandfather, you must not only aim well, but also be able to shoot quickly. If an animal or an enemy moves just when

Small bow with
Blunt Arrow
Itazipa Peconpi

you shoot, you must be ready with a second or third arrow. Aim at the knot again."

Mi'ca and the other boys often played a game of seeing how many arrows they could shoot into the air before the first one fell to the ground. The boy who won could claim an arrow from the one who lost. Mi'ca had won this game enough times to feel confident, so he shot off three arrows as fast as he could and Grandfather looked at him approvingly. "Yes, it is time for you to have a man's bow and arrows, Mi'ca."

Mi'ca's eyes were shining as he looked at Grandfather, but he tried not to show his excitement. He stood quietly and tried to hold himself straight and tall.

"We will make your bow and arrows together, " said Grandfather. "I will teach you as my father taught me and soon you will be able to make them yourself."

Grandfather put aside his work, went into the tipi, and brought out a bundle of wood for bows. "My favorite wood is a young ash tree killed by a prairie fire, that wood will be seasoned and not affected by rain or damp weather. But, many other woods are good if they are strong and flexible." He untied the bundle and spread the sticks out before Mi'ca.

Mi'ca saw one piece of wood that had an unusual silvery color. "Would this make a good bow for me, Grandfather?" mi'ca asked.

Grandfather flexed the wood slightly between his hands. "Yes, it has a lot of spring in the wood and you will be able to shoot quickly with it. Now, a good bow must always be the right length in proportion to your body. Hold one end of the stick at your right hip and stretch out your left hand at the height of your shoulder. The other end of the bow should be where the wood touches your finger tips.

Black Ash
Pse'htin

Ash wood was used for making bows. A small straight tree without knotholes was cut when the sap was down, preferably at the end of winter. The piece of bow wood was rubbed with bear grease. Several of such sticks were then bound together with rawhide strips so they would not warp. They were hung high on a tipi pole so that the smoke from the fire would cure the wood.

Grandfather cut the piece to the right length, and then with a knife he began to shave off curls of wood. He showed Mi'ca how to alternate the work from one end to the other. "If you finish one side and then go to the other it will never be as finely balanced as when you keep changing sides and take off equal amounts on each end."

Mi'ca tried to imitate his Grandfather's long easy strokes, but it was hard to do and the knife often caught in the wood. Grandfather was very patient with him and encouraged him with each stroke. Just when Mi'ca felt he was doing well, Grandfather took the bow from him to inspect it. He scraped a bit here and there and then handed it back to Mi'ca along with a sandstone to polish it. The polishing was more difficult and it took them until late in the afternoon to rub and smooth the bow. "Before we stop for the day," Grandfather said, "I will put a notch on the end to keep the bowstring in place. Then you can cut the notch on the other end." When both notches were made, Mi'ca picked up the bow and felt it. He was terribly pleased with his man sized, silvery bow. Standing very solemnly before his Grandfather he thanked him for teaching him and helping him to make such a beautiful bow.

Grandfather stood up and turned towards the setting sun and Mi'ca rose to stand beside him. Then very quietly Grandfather said, "The rays of the sun, Wi, have passed here and touched our dwelling and left their warmth, touching each one of us." Then he smiled at Mi'ca. Mi'ca couldn't remain solemn any longer. He broke into a wide grin and gave his grandfather a tremendous hug.

The hunters left the camp with the first light of morning and just as the birds began to call. The rest of the people went down to the river to bathe. But when the sun, Wi, rose above the horizon all the people stopped what they were doing to watch in silence. After the sun had risen Mi'ca and his friends were soon yelling and

Bow
Ita'zipa

Arrow
Wanhin'kpe

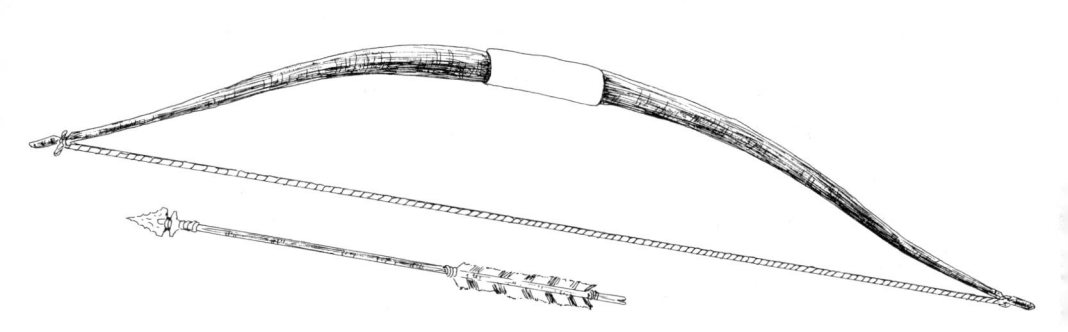

Bow
The thickest part is at the center where the bow is grasped. It is tapered to the ends and notches are cut to hold the bowstring. The bowstring is permanently tied at one end and has a loop at the other end to slip into the notch. When not in use the loop is slipped off and the bow lies flat.

Arrow
The arrow shafts must be cut when the summer growth has ended. They must be straight and smooth and not quite so thick as one's little finger, and 2 to 2 1/2 feet in length. They are tied in bundles of 20 - 25 and wrapped tightly with strips of rawhide. The bundles are hung high above the fire on a tipi pole to season for several weeks. When they are taken down the bark is scraped off and the shafts are cut to the correct length.

splashing one another until they became hungry and started to walk back to their tipis. Mi'ca remembered to look for animal tracks, but by then the boys footprints had obliterated any sign of them.

    Mi'ca ate hurriedly so that he could get back to finishing his bow. He felt really proud that he was learning skills that would help him to be a good hunter. When he got to Grandfather's tipi he found Grandfather putting some bear grease on the ends of the bow. He held one end over the low fire until it was hot. Then he put that end on the ground and held it down with his foot and began to bend the bow, holding it until the wood had cooled and had a permanent curve. He had Mi'ca do the same to the other end. They were only slight curves, but they would help the bow bend properly when it was strung.

    Grandfather made some glue by boiling small chips of rawhide and a buffalo hoof. "We need to glue a strip of buffalo hide on the back of the bow to give it strength, and another around the grip so that you can hold it comfortably. For the bow string we will use a tightly twisted sinew and tie that permanently on one end of the bow. On the other end we will make a loop that can be slipped into the notch you have made for it. Be sure that when you are not using the bow, you always slip the loop off so that the bow will lie flat. If you keep the wood bent it will become weak, and your arrows will not have enough speed to kill your game. Besides, it is the only way you can carry it in your quiver. Now, one more layer of glue over the whole bow before we hang it up to dry."

    Tato'ka came into the tipi while they were working and when he saw the silvery bow he admired it at once. He asked Mi'ca if he would go with him into the woods when he was finished. He wished to talk to him more about the Vision-quest and perhaps they could find some game to bring back to the tribe. Mi'ca smiled at his uncle and nodded his assent.

When they left the encampment Tato'ka turned and led the way down a game trail. They walked single file without talking until they crossed a small brook. On the other side was a large flat rock. Tato'ka sat down and motioned Mi'ca to sit beside him.

"Of course, you know much about the Vision-quest, and have discussed it many times with your friends, but now that you will soon be going on yours, we should go over the details together. You know that you will have to go away from the camp and stay alone for three days. During that time you must not eat or drink anything." Mi'ca felt a thrill of excitement that he was finally being instructed and prepared for his manhood trials - and he felt a little scared also. The Vision-quest was so important.

"As you sit alone you should think about Wakan-tanka, the Great Mystery. You should feel how your life fits into the great world of nature all around you. You must think about Inyan, the Rock, the ancestor of all things. He stands for authority, as well as for all the beautiful things we make with our hands. His color is yellow. Maka, the Earth, from which all things grow, has the color of green. Wi, the Sun, is all-powerful and will help you to be brave and strong, to be generous and to be faithful. His color is red. Skan, the Sky, is blue. He caused all things to be made in fours: the four directions, West, North, East and South. Time has four parts: day, night, month, and year. Above the earth there are four elements: The Sun, the Moon, the Sky, and the Stars. The plants have four parts: roots, stems, leaves and fruit. There are four kinds of animals: crawling, flying, four-legged and two-legged. Man's life also has four parts: infancy, childhood, manhood, and old age. Skan also caused everything to be round. The Sun, the Moon, the Earth, and

Arrowhead
Wanhi

Arrow nock
Wahinkpe

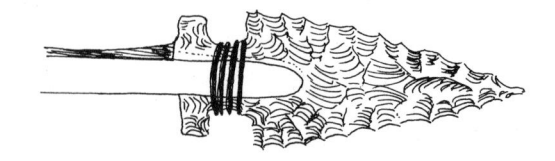

The shaft is split at the end and the arrowhead is slipped in. Both the shaft and arrowhead are then bound together with sinew.

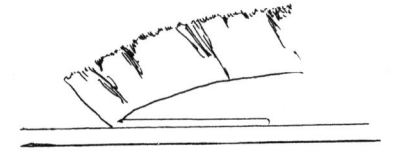

Shaft
Wansaka

Feather glued to shaft

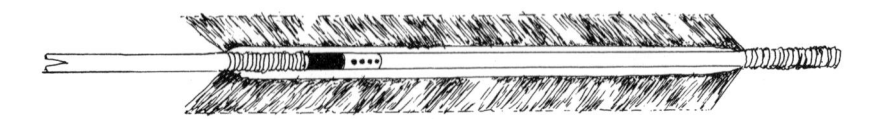

The feather is lashed down with sinew which is first soaked in water. When the sinew dries it shrinks and binds the feather to the shaft.

Owl, hawk, turkey or eagle feathers were preferred. They were first soaked, then split in half and most of the quill removed. The feathers were cut 6 to 8 inches long and three of these split feathers were used on each arrow to give it balance.

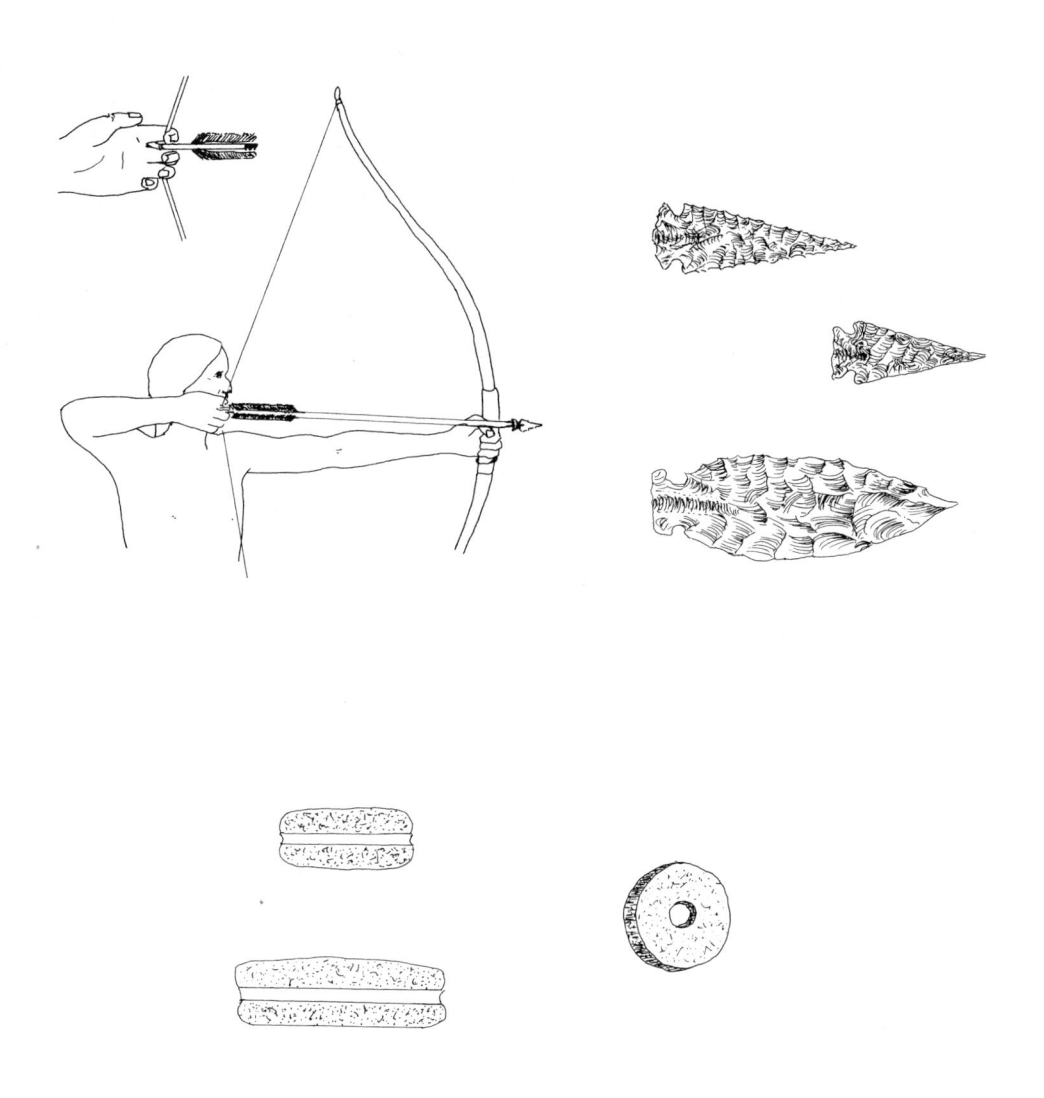

Arrow Straighteners

If the arrowshaft is not straight it can be rubbed with bear grease and warmed over a fire and then pulled through a grooved stone, or a stone with a round hole in it, called arrow straighteners. Since it often took a whole day to make an arrow, it was worth the time to keep it straight.

the Sky are round. The Sun and Moon circle the Sky. The Winds circle the edge of the World. The stems of plants and the bodies of animals are round. The Circle is a sacred symbol to our people and four is our sacred number. All of these things together and much, much more make up our Great Spirit, Wakan-tanka.

"You must think about all the birds and animals, for they are the messengers between us and the spirits surrounding us. In your dreams your spirit will go forth from you on an adventure. The first animal which appears to you in your dream-vision will be your spirit protector throughout your life. You can call upon his spirit to help you at any time. You may return to our camp only *after* you have found your protector.

A shadow fell over Mi'ca. He looked up to see a large eagle flying overhead. It made him feel uneasy, but Tato'ka was speaking again.

"When you return to camp your mother will feed you and give you something to drink so that you may regain your strength. When you feel strong enough you must go forth with your bow and arrows and find the animal you have dreamt of. When you have killed it you must carefully remove the skin and preserve it and keep it with you for the rest of your life. It will be your protector and secret helper."

Mi'ca sat very still. He knew that each brave had his own protecting animal, but no one had ever spoken to him in quite this way about spiritual matters. It made him feel good to think that the tribe trusted him and wanted to count him among the Braves.

His uncle motioned Mi'ca to get up. Have your eyes been sharp enough to notice which animals are about us here in the forest? Is there any meat nearby for us to carry home?"

Mi'ca had noticed prints near the stream bank just before they

Eagle
Wan'bli

sat down on the rock, but, again he had failed to look as closely as he should. He decided to risk a guess. "I think I saw deer hoof prints at the edge of the brook we crossed," he said rather hesitantly.

"Trust your eyes and your ears. They are your helpers. Yes, they were deer prints, and they were made not long ago," Tato'ka said. "We will follow the little trail up to the left. This is a place where the deer like to come down to drink, and they have worn a trail of their own. Now we must stop talking and go to where they are grazing. When we get close breathe quietly and walk putting your toes down first and then let your weight drop onto your heels. Take only a few steps at a time, don't rustle dead leaves and don't step on dry twigs which will snap and alert your prey. Follow me."

Tato'ka moved quickly and quietly away and Mi'ca could hardly keep up with him. The forest was beautiful here with oak trees whose trunks were thick enough to hide behind. It was all very quiet and peaceful. But a bluejay had spied them and had begun a warning call, and that was not good since it alerted other animals. Tato'ka quickly took off his moccasins so that he could feel the ground with his toes and stalk even more noiselessly. Mi'ca, in trying to walk so silently had fallen behind, and momentarily lost sight of his uncle. They had come to the edge of a meadow filled with sunlight. After the shady forest the light was so bright that it took Mi'ca a few moments to see his uncle standing on the other side of the clearing behind a tree. Only then did he see the five grazing deer Tato'ka had seen long before. There was a slight twang and one of the deer dropped. As the other deer looked up in alarm and began running off, a second half-grown deer fell as well.

Tato'ka stepped out into the meadow and motioned to Mi'ca. They went to the deer and pulled out the arrows which could be used again and so were rubbed off on the grass before Tato'ka put

Blue Jay
Zintka togleglega

Pussy Willow
Cohwanzica

them back in his quiver. Tato'ka crouched down, slit the belly of the deer and removed the entrails to make the deer a little lighter to carry back. Then he showed Mi'ca how to do it on the smaller deer. After they had finished Tato'ka pulled the heavy deer up on his back, holding the two front legs with his right hand and the two back legs with his left. He had Mi'ca hang his quiver with its bow and arrows over his head so that it hung on his chest.

"Do you think you can carry the small one on your back?" he asked. MI'ca tried to imitate his uncle's easy movements, but found it far from easy. The animal was very heavy, but he finally settled the weight on his shoulders and they started off for camp. Now they didn't have to be so quiet, fortunately for Mi'ca, as he was soon breathing heavily because of the weight. At the brook Tato'ka leaped across first and laid the animal down, and then took Mi'ca's load and brought it across as well. Tato'ka thought they should rest a bit, so they sat again on the flat stone and watched the sunlight sparkle on the water until they felt rested. It was a long walk back and Mi'ca had never felt so tired as he did now.

"Drop your meat before the door of your tipi. I will bring mine to my tipi, but since it is larger I will share it with grandfather." And with that Tato'ka went on.

Deer
Tahca

3

The Arrows

Ina (Mother) looked out through the tipi door to see what had made such a thud. When she saw the deer she smiled at Mi'ca and stepped out of the tipi. "My brother is teaching you well. Help me to remove the hide and cut up the meat."

Mi'ca's sister, Mahpi'ya ska (White Cloud) came out behind her mother and swiftly and silently set up some sticks from which she hung a buffalo paunch. She poured in some water and then added pieces of the deer meat as Mi'ca handed them to her. Then with two sticks she carefully picked up a glowing stone from the fire and dropped it into the paunch to cook the meat. She stirred it to keep the stones moving so they would not burn the cooking paunch. Then, she had to remove those cooling stones and add several more heated stones before the meat was cooked. When it was done the three sat on the grass to eat, dipping their horn spoons into the cooking paunch and filling their wooden bowls. Mi'ca was very hungry and very happy.

When Mi'ca went to his Grandfather's tipi the next morning, Grandfather took down a bundle of sticks for arrow shafts and said, "Arrows have to be the right size to fit your bow, and they should all be the same length because arrows of different lengths will fly differently and your hunter's aim will be destroyed. If we measure from your elbow to the tip of your little finger, plus the

Deer
Tahca

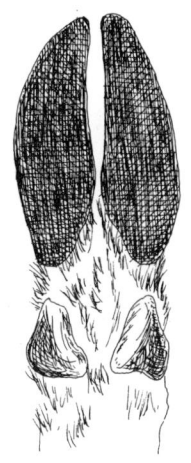

Left front hoof

length of that finger it will be just right. You must keep this shaft as a pattern for all of your arrows, that is unless you suddenly decide to grow still taller!" They cut the shafts and scraped off the bark and then Grandfather showed Mi'ca how to shape the notch in the back to fit the bow string, and a slit on the tip to hold the arrowheads in place.

There was a great deal of commotion to the north of the camp and the dogs began barking. Mi'ca went to see what was happening and found that another band of Sioux had arrived. They were unharnessing their dogs and setting up their tipis. The dogs already at the camp were making this difficult by jumping around and barking at the newcomers. Mi'ca watched for a while, then ran back to camp to tell his friends, but before he reached them Grandfather called to him.

"What have you learned about the newcomers, Mi'ca?" he asked. He nodded as Mi'ca described what he had seen, then smiled and said, "Those are the people who trade with us for our wild rice. They bring us large stones to make scrapers and knives as well as smaller stones for arrowheads. They may even have some pipes which they make of stone. I will put on my buffalo robe and we can go together to greet the newcomers."

They walked to the new encampment and found the Chief sitting cross-legged outside his tipi. Grandfather raised his hand in greeting and said, "Hou!"

The Chief rose to his feet and replied "Hou!"

When they had seated themselves on the ground, Grandfather began, "My grandson, Mi'ca, has come with me today. We seek stones for arrowheads. Have you brought such things with you?"

The chief nodded and called to his wife to bring the sack of arrowhead stones from the dog pack. She hadn't finished unpack-

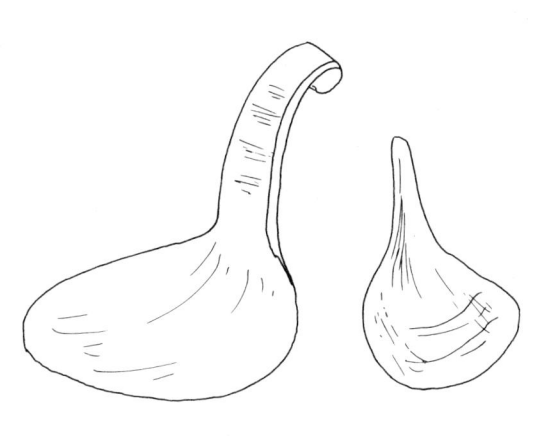

Wooden Bowls
Waksica

Usually carved from hardwood burls.

Horn Spoons
Kinska

Spoons were carved from fresh, pliable horn, boiled first to make it easy to reshape and carve.

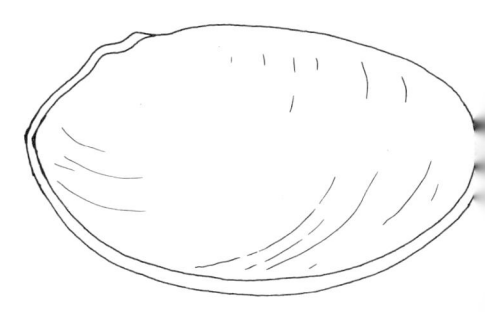

Animal stomach pouches were hung from sticks lashed together. Water and meat pieces were placed inside the pouch and stones heated in a fire were dropped in to cook the meat.

ing the various bundles of robes and clothing and food, so it took her a while, but she soon found the right bundle and brought it over and laid it on the ground before her husband. He picked it up and handed it to grandfather who carefully shook out the stones onto the ground. Mi'ca's eyes opened wide when he saw the many stones of flint, jasper, chalcedony and even some pieces of black and sparkling obsidian. They must have come from very far away.

Grandfather turned over many stones, and put the ones he liked in a pile before him. When he had selected all he wanted he turned to Mi'ca. Mi'ca had just noticed that one particularly interesting stone had rolled near his foot, and asked whether that one could also be taken. Grandfather agreed, and gathered the stones in a corner of his robe. When he stood up too bid the chief goodbye, he told him to come and visit him soon for he had a store of wild rice and cakes of maple sugar for him. This year had seen a good harvest.

When Mi'ca and his grandfather got back to the tipi they laid all the stones in front of them and Grandmother came out to look at them. She often helped Grandfather look for stones, but in the forests there were not many stones suitable for making tools and arrowheads. She brought out some leather pouches and began to sort the new stones before putting them away. Grandfather picked up a flint stone and began to work it into an arrowhead. He chipped first on one side and then on the other. The trick, he told Mi'ca, was to find the right direction to hit it, and the proper force of the blow for that particular stone. He handed it to Mi'ca and watched him as he tried to find the right way to aim his blows. When he had gotten two arrowheads roughed out, Grandfather took it and showed him how to strike out the notches on each side to hold the lashing. Grandfather held the stone with a piece of

Whitetail Deer Fawn
Sinte hanska tacincala

buckskin, so as not to cut his hands on the sharp edges, then picked up a chipping tool made of deer antler. With this he only had to press carefully on the edge with a twisting curving motion to snap off a small chip. He alternated by snapping chips from one side and then the other until the whole arrowhead was perfectly formed. Mi'ca was fascinated by how Grandfather worked. He told him that the way he handled his tools seemed almost like a dance rhythm or a drum beat. Grandfather, pleased to hear that, put down his tools and smiled at Mi'ca, first with his eyes crinkling up, and then with his lips. "Ah, Coyote Cub, you are becoming grown-up in your ways and thoughts. You have noticed one of the important things of life. The tasks you set yourself should be performed with love and care. You must feel the stone and come to know its hardness. You must have the right tools to work with, and as you work you must make your own rhythms to help you in your work. If you sing while you work the rhythm of your chant will help your hand to move with a rhythmic stroke."

Mi'ca tried to sing as he pounded but it wasn't easy and he knew it would take lots of practice to make perfect arrowheads.

The next morning when Mi'ca ran down to the river he realized that he had had little time for play these days, and had hardly seen his best friends. When he mentioned it to them he found that several of them were also being prepared for their own Vision-quest ceremonies, and were as busy as he was in learning how to make bows and arrows and track animals. The boys had seen these things being done around them all their lives, but until now they had not been asked to participate in the work of the men. They were excited by the thought of being able to practice together with real bows and arrows That would change their games from play to real hunting. They felt proud.

Wild Rice

Psin

The rice grows in shallow water. When it is ready to be harvested the stalks are bent over the canoe and the rice grains are beaten out into the bottom of the canoe.

When Mi'ca went back to Grandfather's tipi he found that Grandfather had laid out a row of feathers. "The arrow needs feathers to guide it straight just as an eagle needs tail feathers to enable it to swoop down on his prey," said Grandfather.

They glued three feathers to each shaft and between the feathers they painted bands of color, black for night and red for day. Mi'ca then had to decide what his own mark would be. "Tato'ka told me many things about the number four, so I think I should like to have four black dots on the red band." he finally decided.

"Grandfather," said Mi'ca, "I want to make an especially good arrowhead from the stone I got from the Chief. I want to do it by myself, but will you sit beside me and guide my hand?" Grandfather crinkled up his eyes and smiled at Mi'ca.

When he had removed the outer layer of stone he found that it was as white and shiny as his bow. He searched through the shafts until he found one that matched the bow wood. He was terribly excited. How beautiful they all looked together! He knew immediately that he wanted to put some white turkey feathers on the shaft as well. Grandfather was very pleased when Mi'ca was all finished and the bow and arrow placed side by side. Mahpi'ya walked by and noticed the bow and arrows lying on the ground. "I want to make a quiver case for you, Mi'ca. Your old case will be too small to hold your new bow and arrows, and besides, it's a sister's duty to take care of her brother!" she said with a mischievous twinkle in her eyes. Grandfather smiled at Mahpi'ya and said, "Bring your skins and work on the quiver here so that you can measure it to the right size.

Mahpi'ya brought a big bundle of skins tied together with rawhide thongs. She found a sleek grey otter skin in the pile, and turning it over on the back she marked the size with a piece of

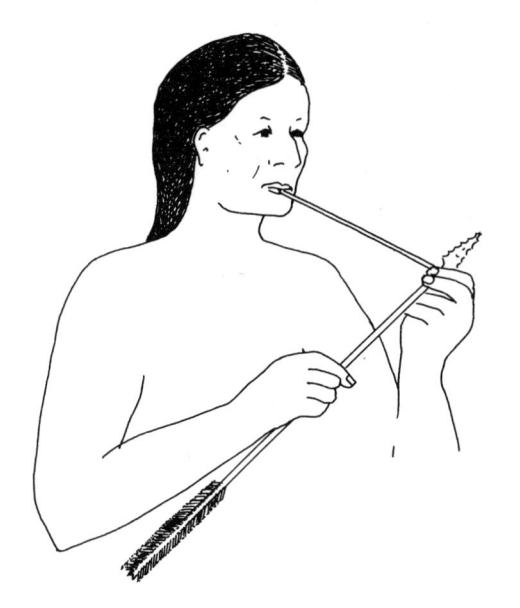

Binding an arrowhead to the shaft with sinew.

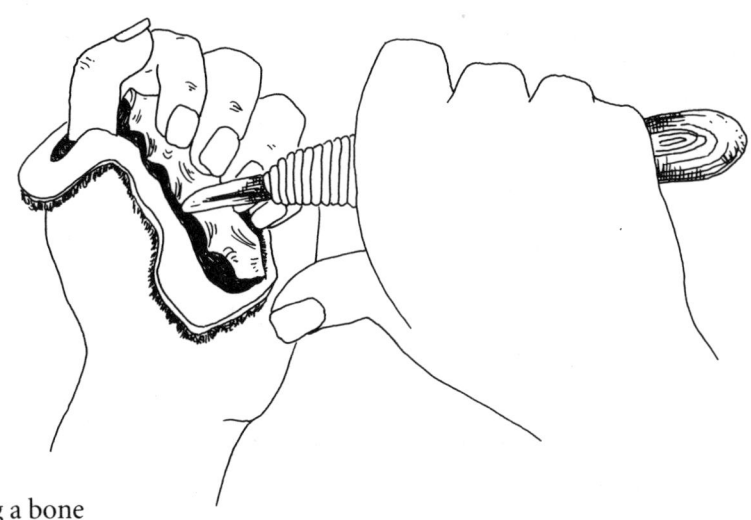

Using a bone flaking tool to shape an arrowhead.

charcoal from the fire. She cut the skin with a stone knife and carefully punched holes along the edges with a sharp bone awl and then she laced the pieces together with sinew.

"While you are both working, let me tell you about the Ancient One," Grandfather began. "In the beginning there was no one but the Old Man. He was not really different from any of us now, but he had powerful medicine and could do astonishing things. First he thought he would like to have a world, so he made this one. It was all flat, and when you came to the edge it went straight down. After he looked at it a long time, he decided that it was too flat. He began walking around on it and then after a while he made some running jumps. At every jump a mountain rose under him. From the mountains he cut gashes down to the plains, and valleys formed and creeks and rivers ran deep in the bottom of them. He liked the way it looked, and decided that there should be living things on it, so he made grasses and trees and flowers. Then he made animals, and finally people. All the people then had paws just like the other animals, but they were quite helpless in the face of bears and animals that were big and strong. So, whenever they wanted to, the other animals killed and ate people. The Old Man was so busy going here and there inspecting his world and the things he had made on it that it was some time before he saw what was happening to the people. When he did notice, he sat down on a big rock and thought for a long time. Finally, he called all the people to him and slit their claws so that they became fingers and thumbs. Then the people could use their hands to do all sorts of work. He showed them how to make bows and arrows, arrowheads and stone knives. Then he taught them how to shoot the animals and cut up their meat and prepare the hides so that they could be used for clothing. Finally he gave them fire. Then they

Basswood
Hinta

The inner bark has a tough fiber which was used for rope. The rope was most frequently used to tie rice bundles.

could cook the meat as well keep themselves warm when the white giant of the North, Wazi'ya, blew his cold winds."

Mahpi'ya had been making a shoulder strap for the quiver and was stroking the soft fur of the quiver sack. She envied Mi'ca. He could go hunting and do brave things, but then she thought of the dangers— like facing bears—and was glad to be making a quiver instead of using it.

Mi'ca asked Grandfather if the bow was strong enough to kill a buffalo, and Grandfather said yes, but it would require a strong arm, and he would need to practice a great deal to become familiar with the pull of the new bow. "You can aim at a piece of hide thrown over a bush, or a ball of grass thrown high in the air. But before you begin to use your bow and arrows we must take them to the Wise One of our camp, Wapi'ya, Healing Medicine, and he must put his blessing on them."

When they reached the tipi of Wapi'ya they tapped lightly on the tent flap before entering. Then they stepped in and went to the back of the tipi where Wapi'ya was seated, behind the fire and facing the tipi opening, the most sacred place. He greeted them with great seriousness and motioned to Mi'ca to lay his things down before him, and for them to be seated. He picked up the pipe of peace and offered it to the Sky and the Earth and then to the four directions; West, North, East and South. Then he lit it with an ember from the fire, drew a puff and handed it to Grandfather, who took one puff and handed it back to Wapi'ya.

He talked a while to Mi'ca about how important one's first real weapons were, how they should be handled with care and reverence—as though Mi'ca didn't know that already!—and how important it was to practice every day with the weapons so that they became a natural part of one's thinking and actions. Then

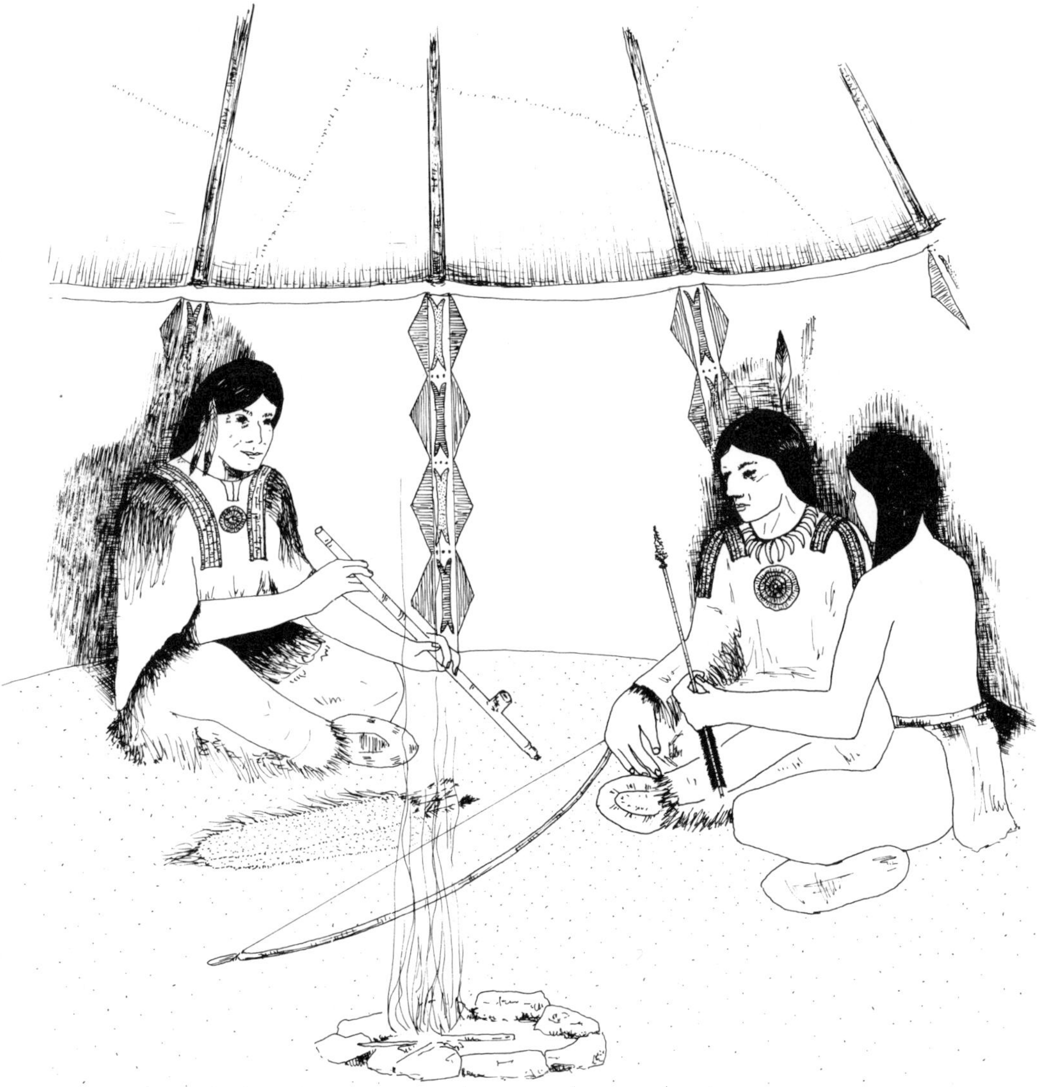

Wapi'ya picked up the bow and felt the strength of it and touched the arrow and quiver case. As his glance fell on the silvery arrow alongside the white bow, a slight shiver passed through his body. He picked up the arrow and held it in his hands. "This arrow has much medicine in it. It speaks to me in a way that I cannot quite understand. I feel that this silver arrow will change your life by some strange and unusual deed that you and it shall perform together!"

White Birch
Canhasan
Tan'pa

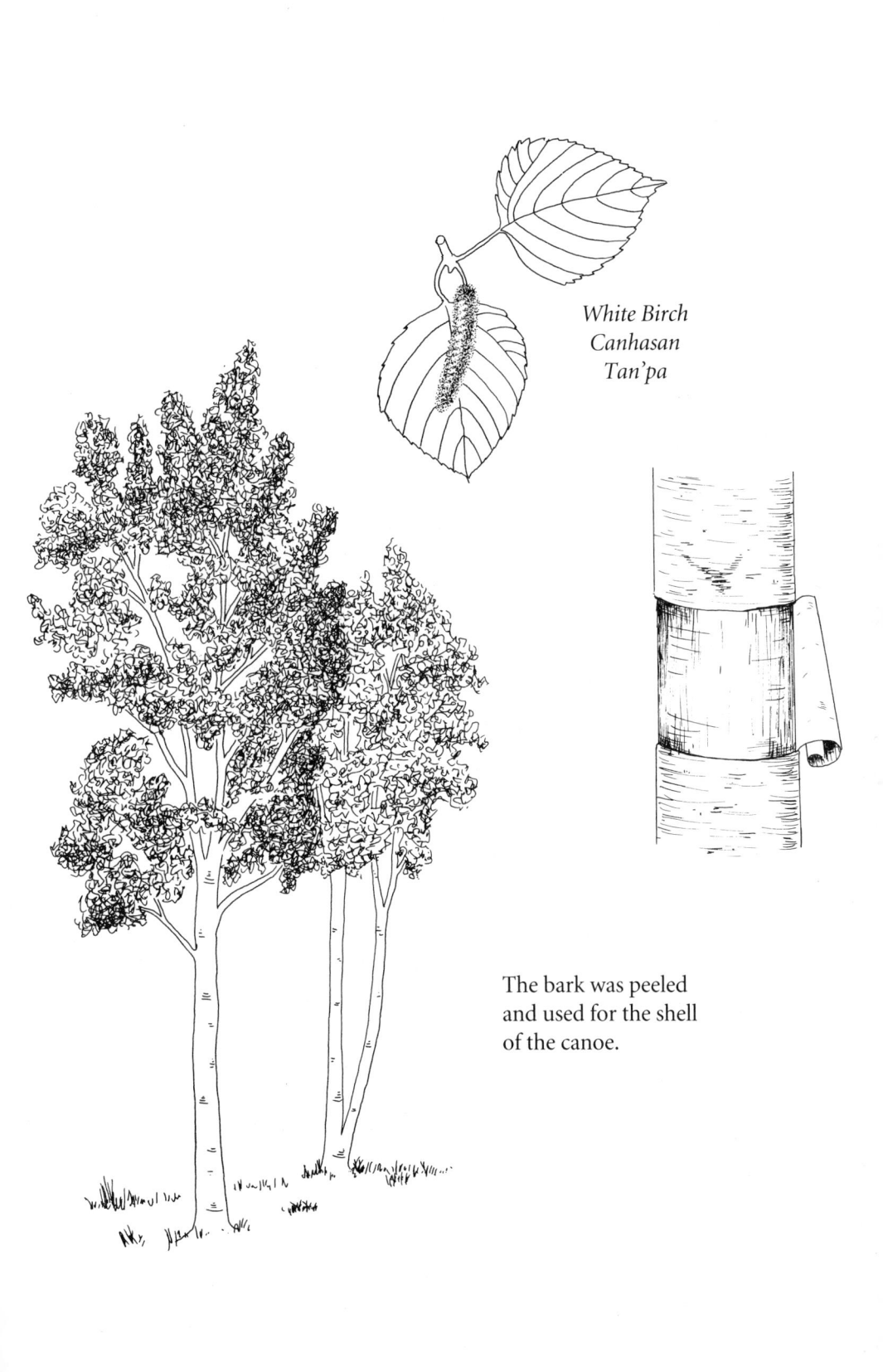

The bark was peeled and used for the shell of the canoe.

4
Moccasins

Mahpi'ya offered to make new moccasins for Mi'ca with porcupine quill work designs on them. She brought out a piece of rawhide which had formerly been used at the top of the tipi. It was well tanned from the smoke of the fire. She laid the piece of hide on the ground and when Mi'ca placed his foot on it she drew an outline with charcoal slightly larger than his foot.

Tato'ka came by just then and crouched down beside them.. "It is time you learn to read the signs of the moccasins," he said, "from them you can tell who has passed by, whether friend or enemy. I will draw in the dirt the shape of the tribes who live near us: the Cheyenne, the Arapaho, the Crow, and the Pawnee. Both of you, Mi'ca and Mahpi'ya, must learn these shapes well, for it is as important to know the tracks that a man makes as it is to know the tracks of an animal. Of course, you might be able to trick an enemy by capturing some of their moccasins and wearing them when you are near his camp so that he will not suspect you of spying on him. Sometimes scouts add a fringe which drags from the heel and blurs the outline of the footprint."

Mi'ca and Mahpi'ya were studying the outlines and trying hard to remember which pattern went with which tribe, when Ina stood up and said that she needed more quills and it was time for Tato'ka to take Mi'ca on a porcupine hunt.

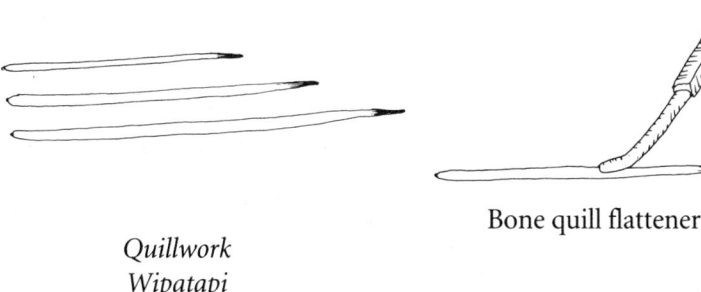

Quillwork Wipatapi

Bone quill flattener

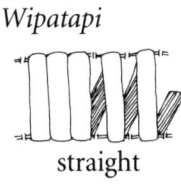

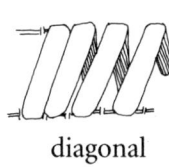

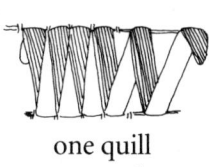

straight   diagonal   one quill crossed

Moccasin Hanpa

Dakota

Cheyenne

Arapaho

Pawnee

Crow

Hide which had once been used for the top of the tipi made good soles because it was well tanned from the smoke of the cooking fire and would not shrink or harden.

The tops of the moccasins were made from soft buckskin. Designs were drawn on with charcoal and sinew was threaded through holes which had been made with a small bone awl.

The porcupine quills are white with a small dark tip. They were often dyed to make colorful patterns. When they were boiled with sunflower petals they turned yellow. Wild grapes turned them black and buffalo berries turned them red. The longer they were boiled the darker the color became. Once the quills were dyed they were flattened with a bone tool or drawn through the teeth of the quill worker. The quill was placed on the leather and a small stitch taken over it to hold it in place. The quill was then bent over the stitch down to the next row. Another stitch was taken to hold it in place and the quill was bent back up to the first row. After two or three turns a new quill had to be added. The ends were tucked under the design to hide them and hold them in place.

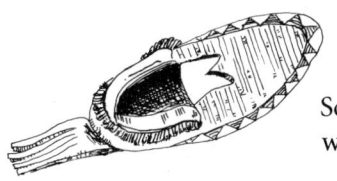

Scout moccasin with drag fringe

Tato'ka looked over at Mahpi'ya and said, "You must come too. Porcupines are often close to our campsites and you should know how to handle them. His footprint is deep because he is a heavy animal, and his claws are very long to help him climb trees. He likes to eat buds and bark, but when he is on the ground he walks with a rolling gait and his tail brushes the ground just as though it had been swept"

The three of them walked towards the forest, looking in every hollow log and heap of branches. When they pushed some bushes aside roughly, Tato'ka called to them to move more cautiously so as not to touch a porcupine by mistake, because the quills came out very easily when the porcupine lashed out at an enemy.

Mahpi'ya was standing very still and listening to Tato'ka when she heard a faint gnawing sound and saw a slight movement out of the corner of her eye. There, some distance away, was a porcupine chewing on a deer antler. A moment later one of the dogs from the camp noticed the porcupine too, and made a rush at it, barking wildly. A kind of grumbling noise came from the porcupine who didn't want to be disturbed in the least. He looked up and made a kind of clicking warning noise with his teeth but this didn't deter the dog.

He was a young dog who had never tangled with this kind of animal before. The older dogs left porcupines strictly alone! As soon as the dog got close enough, the porcupine spun around so that its rear faced the oncoming dog, then he arched his back and began thrashing out with his tail. In a moment, dozens of quills were embedded in the nose and mouth of the startled dog who began howling with pain and pawing at his muzzle. Tato'ka grabbed a heavy stick and rushed to the porcupine. But the porcupine was very quick and spun around, putting his head down under him.

Porcupine
Pahin

There may be as many as 30,000 quills on one porcupine. The quills are white with black or dark brown sharply pointed tips. When used to decorate garments the quills can be left white, dyed with earth colors, or boiled with various plants to give them color.

Tato'ka handed the stick to Mi'ca and together Tato'ka and Mahpi'ya tried to distract the animal so that Mi'ca could strike a blow directly on his head. A blow anywhere else would not have killed him.

Tato'ka then turned his attention to the howling dog who was moaning and dancing with pain. He grabbed the dog around the chest with his left arm, holding him tightly to his body while he took each quill and gave a mighty jerk to dislodge it. Each quill had a sharp tip and tiny scales down its length which stuck in its victim like a barb on a fishhook. If they were not removed quickly, they had a way of working farther and farther into the skin. When the job of pulling out the quills from the dog's nose was finished the dog went whimpering back to camp, shaking his head. Mi'ca, Mahpi'ya, and Tato'ka all let out a sigh of relief and then burst out laughing. Very carefully Tato'ka picked up the porcupine by the front foot and carried him back to camp.

"Hai-ee! That was quick work!" said Ina in surprise. She took a few of the leather scraps left over from making the soles of the moccasins and wrapped them around her fingers so she could pull out the long quills which they would use to decorate the moccasins. When she had removed enough quills they skinned the porcupine and cut up the meat and put it in the cooking pouch. They invited Tato'ka, his wife, and Grandmother and Grandfather to come and share the meal with them, because everyone liked porcupine meat.

When they had finished eating, Mahpi'ya brought out a soft piece of buckskin for the tops of the moccasins and drew an outline wide enough to cover the top of the foot. She picked up a charred stick from the fire and began to draw an arrow for her design on each piece of buckskin. When she had sorted the quills

Butterfly
Kimi'mila

Prairie Aster
Wahcazi wastemna

by color she began her design, but by then the quills had become stiff and hard to fold over, so she put them in her mouth to soften them as she worked. She looked so funny with the sharp points of the quills sticking out of her mouth that Mi'ca began to tease her until she lunged at him. Remembering the howling dog, Mi'ca relented and began to help by sorting quills.

It took a long time for Mahpi'ya to fill in her design, but when it was all done it looked very neat and pretty. When she cut the tongue of the moccasin she made it long with two points. These would be the "Wolf Ears" which would stand up when he wore them. "Now, if you become lost, the wolf ears might help you to find the right trail," she teased.

It took more than a day to make the moccasins, but when they were all finished and Mi'ca put them on Ina said that the Earth, Maka, would be very pleased with these moccasins. For, when one walked, one was bound to crush the grasses or flowers beneath one's feet, but if the moccasins were decorated as beautifully as the flowers one stepped on, then Maka would not become angry.

Sugar Maple
Canhasan

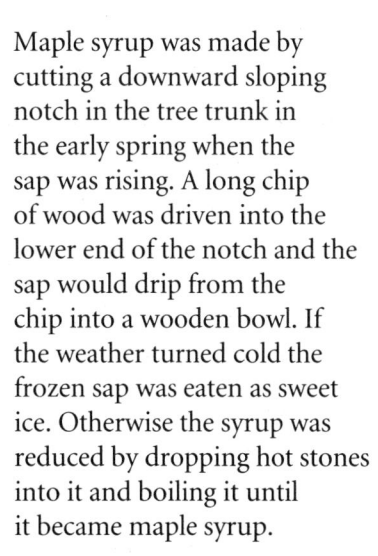

Maple syrup was made by cutting a downward sloping notch in the tree trunk in the early spring when the sap was rising. A long chip of wood was driven into the lower end of the notch and the sap would drip from the chip into a wooden bowl. If the weather turned cold the frozen sap was eaten as sweet ice. Otherwise the syrup was reduced by dropping hot stones into it and boiling it until it became maple syrup.

5

Vision-quest

Tato'ka came almost every day to instruct Mi'ca. At first the new bow felt heavy and was hard to pull, but Tato'ka showed him how to grasp the bow to give it the best balance, to stiffen and straighten his arm as he pulled back on the bowstring and to watch for that exact moment when he should let the arrow fly to its target. At first they practiced close to the camp and shot at an old piece of hide which had been thrown over a bush. but as Mi'ca's arm became stronger he could shoot more quickly and more accurately. Tato'ka now took him deeper into the woods and they trailed real game. This was one of the most exciting things Mi'ca had ever done. Tato'ka was a patient teacher, even when Mi'ca had become so enthusiastic about the chase that he rustled some leaves and startled the game, or shot too quickly for fear that he would not shoot quickly enough. Tato'ka had had his own bow ready and if Mi'ca's shot missed its target, Tato'ka's shot usually brought it down. Little by little Mi'ca got better and more confident and quite often it was his arrow which found it's mark. It was not long until Mi'ca was left to practice by himself or go to the woods with group of other boys who would soon be counted as men of the tribe. They were all bright eyed with enthusiasm at their new status among the men of the Wahpeton.

In the season when the wild strawberries were just blooming,

White Oak
Utahu

Acorns were ground into a meal, boiled and eaten as mush.

Tato'ka appeared at the tent doorway just before dawn. Mi'ca got up and stepped outside to greet his uncle, thinking that they would be going on an early morning deer hunt. But, instead, Tato'ka looked at him with great seriousness and said, "It is time for your Vision-quest. Follow me"

Mi'ca closed the tent flap and tried not to wake his mother and sister, but he suddenly felt nervous. When he looked up, Tato'ka was no longer there beside the tipi. It was hard to see anything in the half-light, but finally he saw Tato'ka waiting for him at the edge of the forest. Tato'ka immediately moved off, quickly melting into the shadows of the trees. Mi'ca ran to catch up with him, but it was all he could do to catch a glimpse of him far ahead. Tato'ka walked with an easy grace holding himself tall and hardly making a sound. Mi'ca felt clumsy by comparison and he was glad that it was getting lighter so that he could see where he was stepping.

They walked in this fashion until almost sunrise, with Tato'ka always far in the lead. Just before the sun rose, Mi'ca saw that they were approaching a high rock outcropping. When he looked up he saw his uncle standing on top. Mi'ca scrambled up the rock and stood beside Tato'ka. As the sun came above the horizon his uncle held his hands up toward and sun and cried "Hi, Hi! The rays of the sun, Wi, come over the land and touch us and give us strength." After a while Tato'ka brought his hands down, looked at Mi'ca and said, "Do not eat or drink anything. Remember that all things in this world have spirits. The sky and the clouds have spirits, the sun and the moon have spirits. Animals, trees, grass, water, stones, all have spirits. These spirits surround us and help us. We must always remember to live in harmony with all of nature. It is very important for us to pay attention to how we communicate with all living things for all of nature watches us just as we watch all of

Greeting the Sun, Wi
Anpo wihinape kiyugate

nature. The spirits will help you and watch over what you do. You must learn to always think before you act and to treat with reverence the unseen forces surrounding you, for they will be trying to lead you correctly. When the Great Spirit, Wakan-tanka has sent you a vision of your protector animal, only then may you return to the tribe." With that he turned quickly, climbed down the rocks and vanished into the forest.

"Involuntarily, Mi'ca's body gave a slight shiver as he began to realize the great responsibility of becoming a man of the tribe. He was not nearly as excited as he had anticipated. Tato'ka's speech had made him feel solemn, if anything. He sat on the rock for a long time thinking of what his uncle had said. When he looked again at the sun a thin haziness had drifted across it. To the west specks of clouds were crowding together, looking like scales on a fish. On the horizon they had crowded into a solid mass of dark grey. Instead of being able to concentrate on the wondrous powers of the sun all he could think of was how soon the clouds would be covering it. He wrapped his arms around his knees, for the air was turning chill and he had on only a breech cloth. He was tired from the early rising and the long walk to the rock outcrop. He began to doze.

When he woke again, the sun had disappeared completely behind the clouds. He tried to smell if there was rain in the air, but decided it was still a long way off. He felt hungry and thought about the hot stew cooking by the tipi fire. Why hadn't Tato'ka given him more specific instructions about what he was supposed to do? Was he supposed to stay in this one spot for three days or was he free to move about? It didn't seem very sensible to stay here on top of the rock if there was a heavy rain coming. He looked again at the steadily darkening sky and decided that it might be

Robin
Bleza

better to find a dry place to sleep for the night. He scrambled down from the rock outcropping and continued on a small trail, but found the land getting rockier and more barren.

Soon the sky was so dark that he couldn't see the sun's position and could only guess in which direction he was now travelling. He felt the first drops of rain on his arm and began to look in earnest for shelter. His eyes searched the rocky outcroppings and finally behind a leafy bush he saw what looked like a cave opening. He scrambled under the overhanging rock just before the rain began. Only once he was inside did he realize that this might be a bear's den. He tensed and sniffed the air as he peered into the darkness. There was a peculiar odor but it was faint and Mi'ca relaxed. He thought perhaps there had been a bear here in the winter, but it was gone now.

He crawled back to the cave entrance and sat and watched the rain. It was coming down steadily now. The rocks around him glistened and the spring flowers bent under the weight of the raindrops and gave off tiny sparkles of light. The smell of the freshly dampened earth released the tenseness in his body and Mi'ca could finally think of being at one with nature. He smiled thinking of Tato'ka's words. He gave a sigh of relief to have found such a comfortable, dry spot.

For the remainder of the day he sat at the cave entrance and watched the wind toss the tree branches to and fro. The small birds hopped from branch to branch, fluffing out their feathers to shake the water from them. Only the robins seemed to be really enjoying the rain because then the earthworms came to the surface, and with a quick tug they had the worms out of their holes and were able to fly off with them to their nests where Mi'ca knew that hungry baby birds waited with open beaks. Mi'ca felt at peace in

Tamarack
Sin'ta

The thread-like roots (Wa'tap) were used to sew the birch bark canoes together.

this quiet spot. Just before night fell he could hear the last calls of the birds and then all was quiet. Mi'ca crawled farther back into the cave and laid down. He fell asleep immediately.

When he woke at dawn the sky was still overcast, but the rain had stopped. A chilly mist filled the air and Mi'ca had no warming fire to sit bedside or food to fill his hungry stomach. He sat up suddenly as he realized that he had had no dream. Well, no need to panic. He still had two more nights, but the thought made him restless. He climbed above the cave and listened to the birds. Their enforced quiet during the rain had made them doubly active in looking for food and staking out their claims to hunting territories this morning. Mi'ca listened to their calls for a while but then turned and walked farther on and eventually came to a deep gorge with a river at the bottom. He cupped his hands and called "HO HA" and the echo was so strong that it made him jump.

Across the river a small waterfall spilled over the canyon wall, but below where he stood there was a sandy beach. The rock walls were sandy yellow and pale grey and seemed to have been worn down in horizontal ridges by waters of ages long past. Mi'ca climbed down the cliff by hanging onto bushes and finding footholds in rock crevices. The bushes which grew close to the water were densely foliaged. Some of the branches even drooped into the water and were pulled along by the current. Mi'ca thought again of Tato'ka's reminder of the forces of nature. He wondered if the bushes liked the feel of the water tugging at them.

It was getting to be evening now and the sun came out briefly just before it set, making an orange glow on the rocks. When the light faded Mi'ca curled up on the still warm sand and fell asleep. He woke once in the night at the sound of an owl's cry and the squeak of some animal the owl had caught. He shivered in the cool

Great Horned Owl
Hinhan'sa

Spies imitated the who-who-who-sound to indicate that an enemy was near.

night air and wished that he had been allowed to bring his sleeping robe, but he curled up more tightly and finally dropped off to sleep.

When he awoke the sun was already far above the horizon. Mi'ca stood up. How could he have slept so long! His stomach growled with hunger and his lips felt parched. He looked at the river and longed to drink his fill of the cool water. Could he bathe? He had been warned not to eat or drink, but nothing had been said about bathing and he was sure it would make him feel better. He stepped into the stream but found that the water ran swift and deep and it would be unsafe to swim here. He splashed a bit of water over his arms and face and then stepped out of the stream.

He thought of the force of the water and wondered if the spirit of the water was a playful one. The sunlight made the surface dance and sparkle. Leaves and sticks which had fallen into the water farther upstream were bounding along and sometimes caught in an eddy which made them turn in circles. Mi'ca felt happy to be alone in the canyon, listening only to the rumble of the water and the twittering of the birds. With a start he realized that again he had had no dream. He tried hard not to worry about it but he felt uneasy. Why was he not able to find his spirit helper? Had he made a mistake in not staying quietly in one place on top of the rock? Probably! He decided to go back to the rock and try all over again. When he climbed up the ravine wall he came out at a different place and when he pushed his way through the underbrush there was no sign of a trail.

Mi'ca sat down to rest and watch the large fluffy clouds drift across the sky. He thought of how quietly they moved. Nothing like the river which also moved but was noisy with gurgles and splashes and rarely absolutely quiet. Mi'ca wondered if the cloud

Grizzly Bear
Mato hota

spirits had fun making the white fluffy masses turn into shapes one could recognize. He laughed out loud when he saw one cloud that looked for all the world like a big curly head of a buffalo. But the cloud drifted on and changed shape and more clouds followed.

When he got up again and tried to find the cave, nothing looked familiar. He wished then that he would have had his Vision-quest in his home territory where he knew every animal path. Here he knew only the paths that he and Tato'ka had hunted on, and he was sure that Tato'ka had taken him to an unfamiliar place now on purpose. What was worse was that the sky had been so cloudy that he hadn't been able to check the sun's direction as well as he would have liked. He walked on, but began to feel more and more lost. Was he getting near the camp-site? For a moment he thought he heard voices and could smell the smoke of cooking fires. But he put this thought out of his mind because he was sure his hunger and thirst was making him imagine things.

Mi'ca heard branches snapping and little growls and yips. He moved very quietly towards the noise. Two small bear cubs were playing and tumbling over each other. They were so woolly and round and looked so nice that Mi'ca moved closer and stood there watching them play. Behind the cubs he suddenly heard a scratching noise and then a loud roar. The mother grizzly bear had been raiding a bee hive for honey and now a swarm of bees was attacking her nose and eyes and she was angry and growling with pain. When she saw that Mi'ca was close to her cubs she turned her fury on him.

Mi'ca turned and ran with all his strength, but a root caught his foot and made him stumble. He was panic-stricken. He knew that a Grizzly could run almost twice as fast as he could. Just as he thought he couldn't run any farther, he saw the edge of the camp.

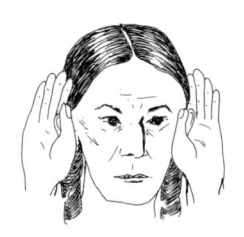

Sign for bear.
Cup hands behind
ears and make a
clawing motion.

Grizzly Bear
Mato hota

Claw
Sake

Mato taoye

In the hope that some scouts were nearby he began to scream "Mato! Mato!" and then he heard an answering shout, "Grizzly! Grizzly!" With his last breath he reached the river and flung himself in, hoping to shake off the bear. As he did so, Tato'ka and three Braves ran past him towards the bear. Several arrows flew at the same time, and the bear dropped in her tracks.

The Braves were very pleased and excited and Mi'ca could hear them exclaiming over the size of the bear. Bear skins were much prized and the meat was good too eat. Tato'ka came back to the still panting Mi'ca and together they went to Grandfather's tipi. There Tato'ka told Grandfather how they had killed the Grizzly almost at the edge of the camp, and Grandfather grunted his approval.

Then they both looked at Mi'ca and asked him about the animal he had dreamed of. Mi'ca hung his head: he had had no dream of any animal. Tato'ka looked shocked. Grandfather looked angry.

"You have returned to the camp before you have fulfilled the Vision-quest?" Grandfather demanded. "You have disgraced us!"

Mi'ca felt the sting of tears in his eyes but fought them back and tried to stand very still with his eyes down. What good would it do to explain that he had been chased by an angry bear, and that he had had little choice in the matter?

"Go to your mother's tipi!" Tato'ka said, with a harshness in his voice that Mi'ca had not heard before.

"There are two small cubs still playing in the forest," Mi'ca finally said in a small voice. Tato'ka nodded, then turned and left without looking at Mi'ca.

Mi'ca backed away from Grandfather, and with a very heavy heart turned towards the trail where the Braves were still cutting the meat from the bear. He made a wide circle around then before going back to his tipi.

Cedar
Hante

The tree rings were split apart and used for canoe frames. the tree was also called "feather leaf" because of the flat sprays.

His mother looked up from her cooking as he approached. She could see that something was terribly wrong. She picked up a ladle and filled Mi'ca's bowl without a word. He took it and ate, but hardly tasted the food. When he was finished he laid down facing the tipi wall and pulled his buffalo robe over his head to hide his shame.

Elm
P'e

The bark fibers can
be twisted and used
for rope.

6
Tangled Hoof

In the morning Mi'ca went down to the river only after the others had left. He didn't want to talk to anyone after yesterday. He swam a while and then sat on the bank brooding. Finally, he stood up and started back to the camp, but then changed his mind and walked along the bank of the river. He was too unhappy to be paying much attention to where he was wandering except that he wanted to get as far away from where he had been yesterday as he could. The sounds of the camp grew fainter as he moved away from the river and towards the open plain.

He picked up a few stones and began throwing them in anger at a group of trees a little way off. The first three missed the trees completely. That annoyed him and pulled him out of his dark thoughts: he should still be able to aim well, even if he hadn't had a vision! Mi'ca picked up a few more stones and threw them hard and straight. The first one hit the tree. The second grazed the trunk and glanced off into the bushes. There was a loud snort of pain from some animal which had been hit by the stone. But what kind of animal made a noise like that? How foolish he had been to go off alone without taking his bow and arrows along! What would he do if something came charging out of the bushes, especially something large? The noise had certainly been made by a large animal. He crouched down and waited, but nothing happened.

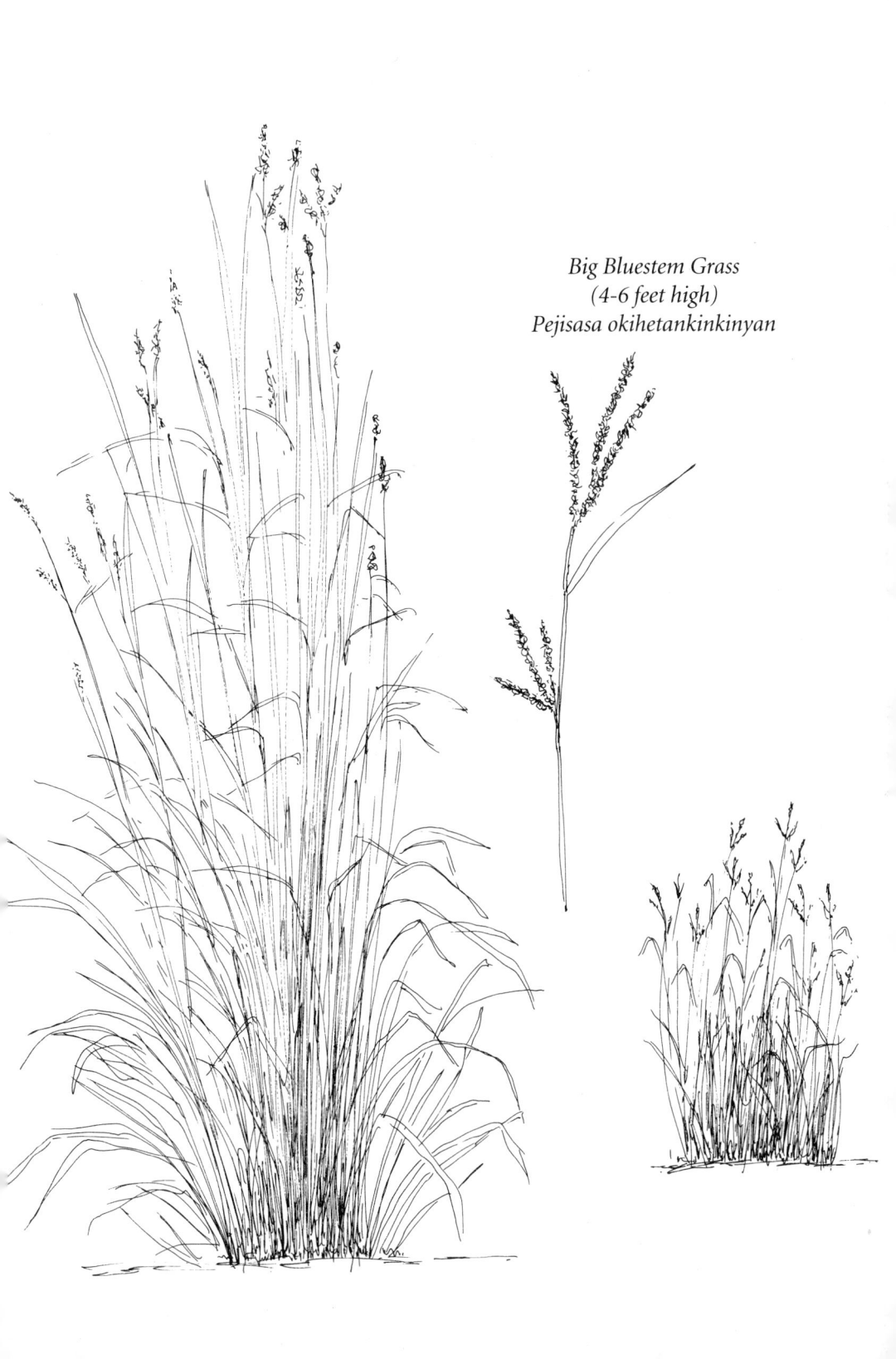

Big Bluestem Grass
(4-6 feet high)
Pejisasa okihetankinkinyan

Cautiously, he moved until he was behind one of the trees in the group he had been aiming at - but the one farthest from the noise. He peered around the trunk, but saw only more trees and dense brush. He tried to put each foot down lightly and slowly so as not to step on a twig or dry leaf while at the same time listening for any sound which would tell him what sort of animal had made that strange snort. He got closer and closer but still couldn't see or hear anything.

He pushed a large leafy branch away and peered past it. He almost cried out in astonishment: there lying in a clearing was a big brown animal. It was bigger than any dog he had ever seen and it certainly wasn't a bear - he didn't think he wanted to see a bear again for a long time. This animal looked a little like a deer, but it was bigger and had a much bigger head - and it had wonderfully big soft brown eyes. Those eyes had been watching for Mi'ca just as Mi'ca had been searching for the animal. After they stared at each other for a moment, the animal tried to push itself to its feet and flee. But Mi'ca saw that something seemed to have entangled one of his hoofs and after a short struggle he became very quiet and settled into the deep grass again.

This animal was magnificent, whatever it was, and it didn't seem especially afraid, just cautious, alert and watchful. Mi'ca edged closer, and then a little closer. The animal didn't snarl or threaten him, and Mi'ca felt braver. After all, it couldn't be very dangerous since the heavy vine entangling its leg was keeping it completely immobile.

Mi'ca couldn't remember anyone ever having spoken of such a beast. Those eyes, big and brown with long black lashes, were very remarkable, but so were the pointed ears and the long nose with the large flaring nostrils which sniffed at Mi'ca. There was a long

White Pine
Wazi

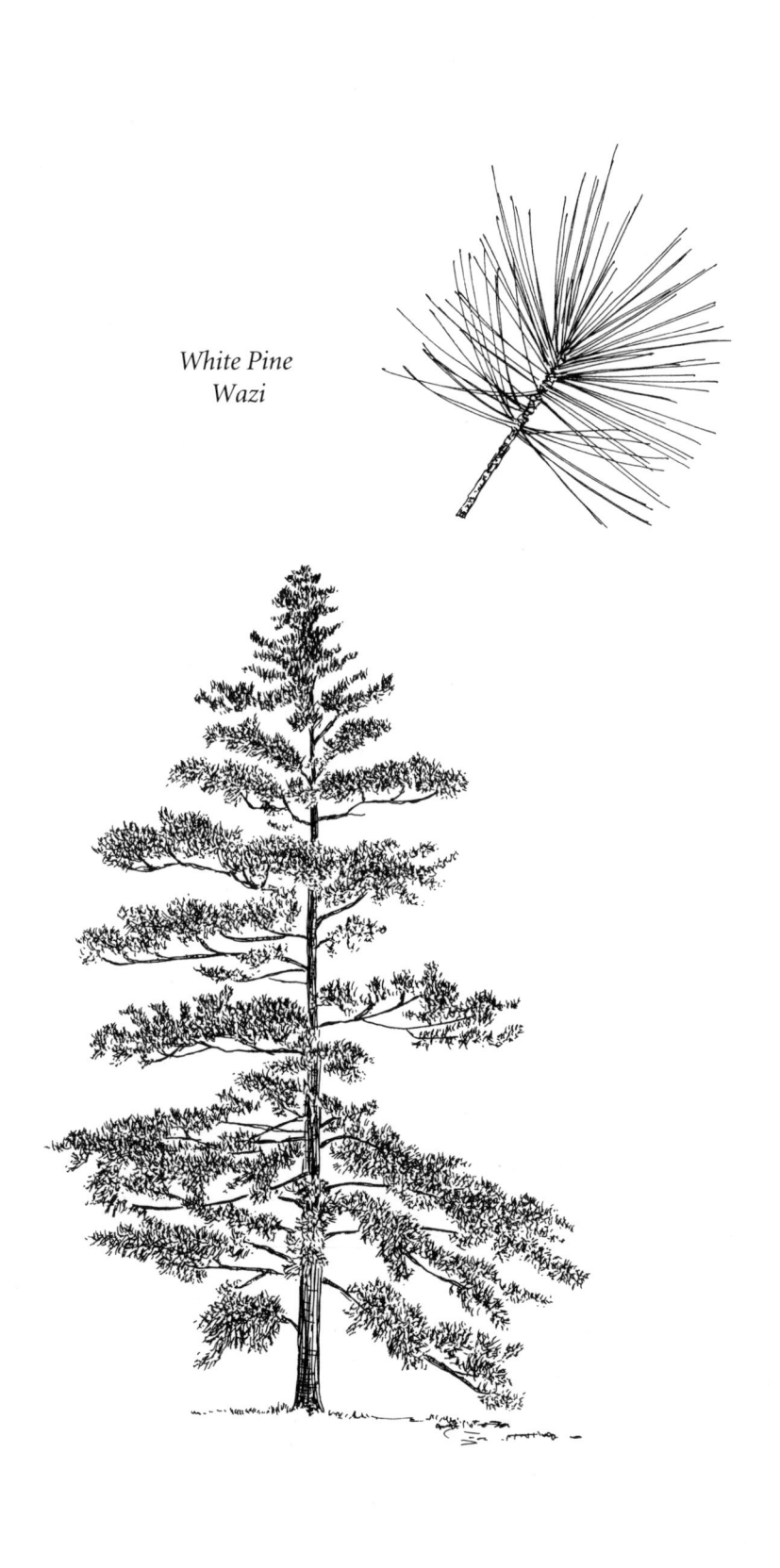

arching neck and a mane of flowing hair from the top of the head down the neck to the back. The mane was dark brown, almost black, and it looked very soft. For a moment Mi'ca wanted to reach out and feel if it was as wonderful as it looked. The body of the animal was big and strong and covered with short glossy brown hair. The legs were longer than a deer's, and there was a long flowing tail. Just above the hoofs the two front legs had bands of white which reached half way the knees.

The more Mi'ca studied the animal, the more he liked him. Without his realizing it, he began to talk softly to it. The animal continued to watch Mi'ca and prick its ears forward as Mi'ca spoke. Then he tossed his head up and shook his mane before he became quiet again. They sat watching one another for a long while. The animal was probably hungry, Mi'ca thought, but what did he like to eat? His jaws and teeth looked like those of a deer and deer liked grass. He looked at the ground around the animal and saw that it had been cropped all around as far as the animal could reach. Mi'ca slowly got to his feet and backed away quietly.

It was quite difficult to move backwards and still not make a sound when you couldn't see where you were going, Mi'ca thought. When he was behind the tree again he looked around for some good long grass and finally saw what he was after out on the prairie. He went and gathered as much as he could carry and returned to the animal. He moved cautiously closer and very slowly laid the grass down, pushing it towards the nose of the animal. To his surprise the animal not only didn't seem frightened, but even started to eat the grass as though he was used to being fed this way. When the whole pile had been eaten, the animal shook his head again and gave a little snort. This was a different kind of snort, a satisfied sound.

Mi'ca was sure that he would want some water to drink, but how was he going to bring that to him? Maybe there was something around the tipi he could use. He backed off again slowly and quietly until he was behind the trees, then turned and went back to the river. He sat and thought. He had two problems: how could he get water back to this strange and wonderful beast, and should he tell anyone about his find? He decided to work on the water problem first. That, at least, was something concrete to do.

When he got back to the tipi his mother looked at him strangely and he hoped she wouldn't ask him questions, but she only inquired if he wanted a piece of dried buffalo meat to take with him to chew on. Mi'ca went over and gave her a big hug and took the jerky from her hand. Then he looked for something to carry water in but could not find anything suitable.

Should he look for his uncle and tell him about the animal? Would his uncle even speak to him now? What if they took a hunting party and shot the animal for food? Mi'ca stopped in his tracks. NO! That would be terrible! All right, that settled it: the animal would have to be Mi'ca's secret, at least until he could figure out how to keep the hunters from finding it.

He wandered over to a big dump pile and there finally saw what he needed. A big dried gourd had been cut in half lengthwise so that it formed a shallow dish, but there was a big crack in it. He picked it up and rubbed the dirt off it and turned it over. Now, how did his mother fix things like this? He almost ran back to the tipi to ask her, but then caught himself. Think! - something sticky and strong, yes, like pine pitch. But there weren't any pines along the river. He would have to go farther away where the soil was drier to find them. He had never felt so impatient about trees, and fairly ran looking for a pine tree. When he finally saw one, it was too

Tall Redtop Grass
Ce'di

Grass tied in bundles to point direction of trail.

young and small to have any pitch oozing out of it.

But soon he did find a whole grove of them, some with sticky pitch on the bark. He smeared the outside of the crack, figuring that it tasted awful. Just to be sure, he tried some - ugh, it really was pretty bad. Now he retraced his steps back to the river and washed his sticky, fingers rubbed them on the grass, then on the stones, then on the grass again to get the pitch off, but some of it just wouldn't come off. He dipped the gourd in the water and lifted it out filled to the brim. It held. He dumped the water out and raced along the bank until he got near to where the animal was.

But, no, it wasn't quite here. Where was it? He ran farther, angry with himself for not paying closer attention to where he had left the stream. Why hadn't he marked his trail by tying a bundle of grass together so that it pointed in the right direction? Then he stopped and told himself he must act like a scout and be calm. He looked at the river, then the trees beside it, then at the trees farther away, and finally he saw the cluster of trees he was looking for. When he got close, he bent down, filled the gourd with water and began to walk back to the animal.

This time it was much harder to be quiet because he had to keep the water from spilling out of the gourd. When he peered through the bushes to find the animal, he found those big brown eyes looking straight at him. Mi'ca wasn't sure how close he could get and still be safe. So he set the gourd down and pushed it towards the nose of the animal. When it was close, the animal stretched his head forward and began to drink. After a few gulps the gourd tipped over and the rest of the water ran out. Mi'ca snatched it up, annoyed, and turned and ran back to the river. In his excitement he had forgotten to be cautious and slow and quiet. Had he frightened the animal?

Coreopsis
Canhlogan wakalyapi

It means "boiled herb" and makes a very good tea.

He filled the gourd again and brought it back. The animal was still watching him, but there was a subtle change in their relation. Mi'ca was no longer afraid and instead of inching slowly along, he just quietly walked over and set the gourd down, but kept hold of the rim so that it wouldn't tip over. Again the animal put his head down and drank, and this time he drank it all. Just as he finished, the animal put his muzzle over and touched Mi'ca's hand with his lip. Mi'ca was so surprised that he pulled his hand away and dropped the gourd. The muzzle had been so soft and so warm. He slowly put out his hand to touch the animal's nose again, and the animal didn't even seem to mind. Mi'ca could hardly believe it. Perhaps you could become a friend of this animal, like you could with a dog, except that this was no dog.

Mi'ca noticed that the shadows were getting longer. He had spent almost the entire day in this little clearing with a creature he had never seen before and certainly had never heard anyone speak about. He decided to gather more grass for him for the night. He went three times to the prairie and brought back big loads each time. He was a little afraid to touch the animal again for fear that he might react differently this time. But before he went, he sat down again in front of the animal to watch him eat. Then he started singing quietly to him about birds and the river and the fleet antelopes.

The animal let out a kind of sigh and his lips fell back in a kind of puff -as though he were contented. Mi'ca instinctively reached out his hand to touch those lips again, but the animal turned his head towards him just then and his hand came down on the nose just above the nostrils. It was hard and bony above, but wonderfully soft below. Mi'ca couldn't resist stroking it again and again. The animal seemed to enjoy it as much as Mi'ca, and both seemed enchanted with each other's company. But it really was getting dark now, and Mi'ca stood up and backed away.

Back in the tipi, Mi'ca had a hard time falling asleep. He kept thinking about those big brown eyes. Had this animal been around people before? He had been frightened at first, but so had Mi'ca. Later on he had seemed unafraid, but still cautious. What would happen now? Should he cut the vine and free him? Would the animal run away? Would one of the hunters see him and shoot him? Should Mi'ca tell someone what he had found? His thoughts swirled around in him until he fell asleep.

When Mi'ca awoke, his first thought was what he could name the wonderful animal he had found. *He* had been named Mi'ca because a coyote cub had come to the edge of the clearing by the tipi in the early dawn when he was born, but what was special about this animal? Well, he had been caught in the vines and couldn't run away so perhaps he should be called Tangled Hoof.

So that no one would begin to wonder what had become of him, Mi'ca began his day as he usually did and set off for the wide spot in the river which made a pool. Many of his friends were already there as was Cha'pa, Old Beaver. Cha'pa was one of the older men of the tribe. He was no longer strong enough to go hunting with the Braves, so he spent much of his time teaching the young people. This was bad luck! Now he would have to stay with the group. Usually he loved to have Cha'pa teach him the tricks of swimming. He especially liked racing with the other boys. He often won even though there were sometimes older and bigger boys racing too.

Today he slid into the water and joined the others. It was a perfect day for swimming. The sun had warmed the water to just the right temperature and the birds were singing their morning songs. Mi'ca floated on his back and looked up at the overhanging trees. But Cha'pa had other things in mind for them and called them together.

"I am not called Old Beaver for nothing," he said. "Today you must learn the ways of the beaver, for he is very intelligent and has much to teach you. When he goes into the water and doesn't want to be heard, he makes his body compact and moves in quietly. This is a good trick to know if there are enemy around and you wish to slip away quietly. Then watch how he swims with his nose just above the water, pushing first one paw and then the other just below the surface. His back feet are large and webbed, and there he has an advantage over you, since they push against the water with more force that you can with your feet, but if you pull your knees up and kick out like a frog, that will make you move more quickly. But remember, these are movements to help you escape your enemy, so you must move quietly. Do not forget yourselves and splash as though you were only playing a game or having a race in the water. You must know the ways of nature, feel the tug of the river current, feel yourself to be a water creature so that you will understand their ways and be like one. Now, one at a time, go quietly into the water and swim like a beaver to the bend in the river where the rock shows above the water. You first, Straight Arrow; next Fox Tail; Two Strikes; Red Plume; Coyote Cub; Elk Horn."

While Mi'ca was waiting for his turn he tried to remember seeing a beaver family playing in a pond. Every once in a while one beaver would chase another round and round, then dive under the surface and the game would be reversed with the chased now the chaser. They had a marvelous time until something alarmed one of the sentry beavers. He slapped the water with his tail with a loud

Beaver
Cha'pa

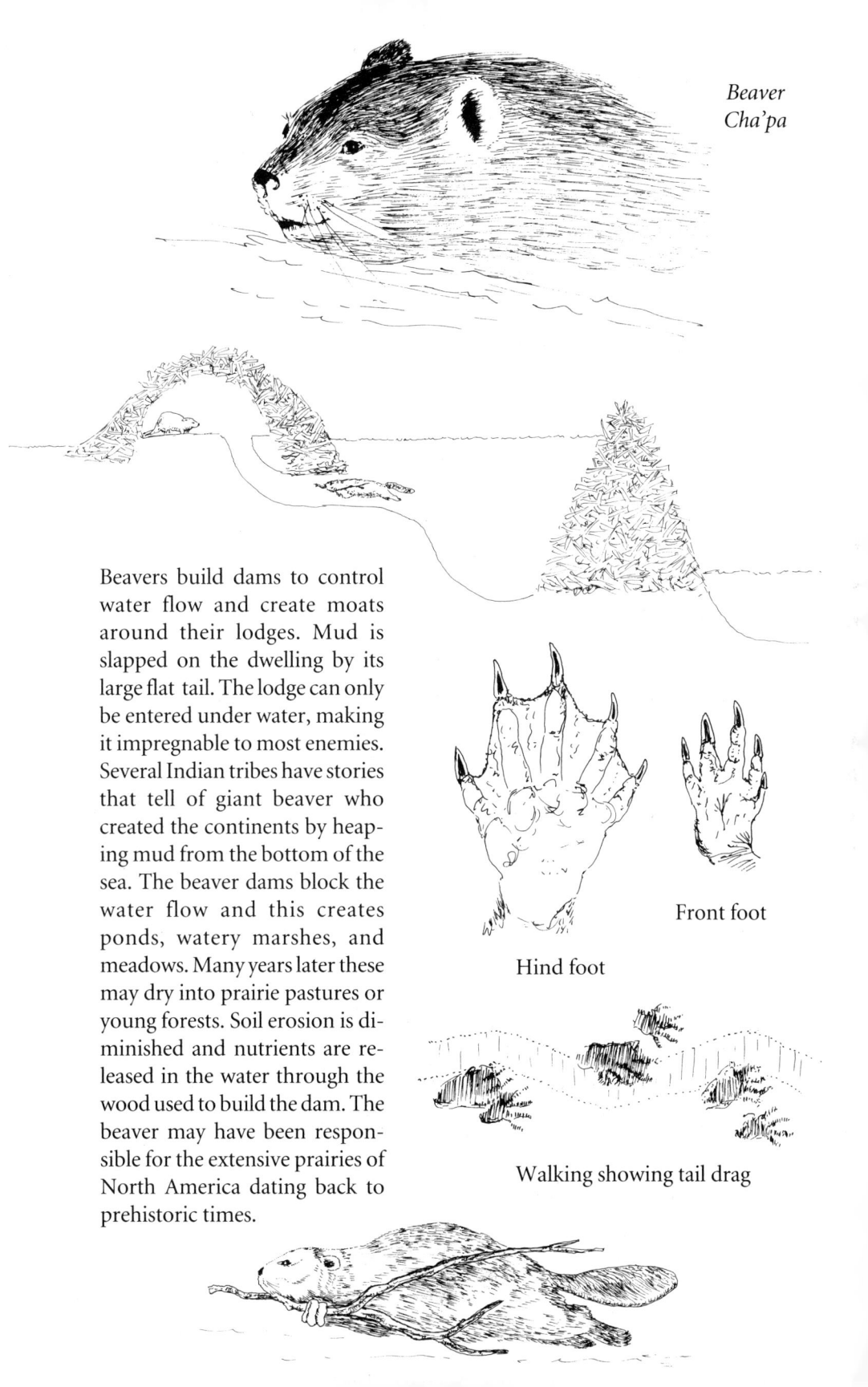

Beavers build dams to control water flow and create moats around their lodges. Mud is slapped on the dwelling by its large flat tail. The lodge can only be entered under water, making it impregnable to most enemies. Several Indian tribes have stories that tell of giant beaver who created the continents by heaping mud from the bottom of the sea. The beaver dams block the water flow and this creates ponds, watery marshes, and meadows. Many years later these may dry into prairie pastures or young forests. Soil erosion is diminished and nutrients are released in the water through the wood used to build the dam. The beaver may have been responsible for the extensive prairies of North America dating back to prehistoric times.

Hind foot

Front foot

Walking showing tail drag

thwack which could be heard from one end of the lake to the other, and every beaver dove below the surface without a sound.

When it was his turn, Mi'ca tried to think like a beaver pretending he had sleek fur which repelled the water and helped him move through the current. Mi'ca liked beavers, they seemed so clever and friendly. The more he thought about them, the easier it was to move like them: quietly and without a ripple.

He gave a little push with his feet and ducked his head beneath the surface, pushing and gliding, trying hard to keep his eyes open under water to watch for the rock. The sunlight filtered through the water and made everything green and at the same time glowing gold near the surface. He saw a trout hanging motionless in a side pool, camouflaging himself. Finally, unable to hold his breath any longer, Mi'ca came up to the surface as quietly as he could and took a breath of air. The current of the river swept him along until he was exactly at the big rock. He hoisted himself up and looked back to where Cha'pa was standing and saw him give a very slight nod of approval.

He climbed up on the rock beside the other boys and shook the water out of his hair. Then he heard one of the boys he had never liked say, "You'd think he would have had sense enough to invent a dream animal before he got back to camp, wouldn't you?" Mi'ca clenched his fists together and lunged toward the tormentor, but the other boys just turned away from him. Mi'ca felt thoroughly shaken and deeply offended at the thought of making up a sacred vision. He turned from the boys and ran back to his tipi, raging inside.

Ina and Mahpi'ya were busy drying wild cherries and buffalo berries in front of the tipi. Ina looked at Mi'ca's troubled, frowning face and told him to go and spend the morning doing what he liked, but in the afternoon she would need his help.

Pemmican Pounder
Wasna icaskice

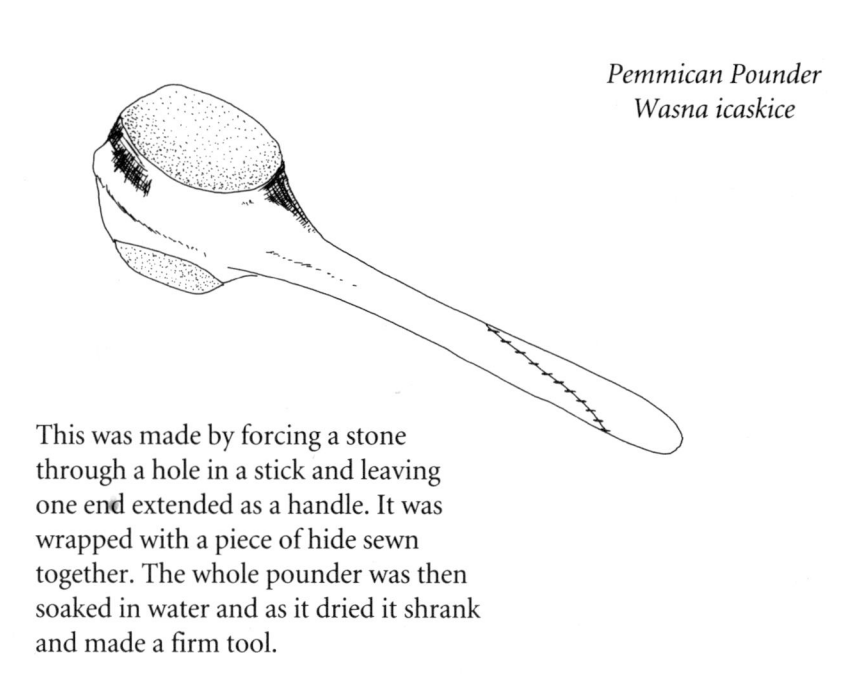

This was made by forcing a stone through a hole in a stick and leaving one end extended as a handle. It was wrapped with a piece of hide sewn together. The whole pounder was then soaked in water and as it dried it shrank and made a firm tool.

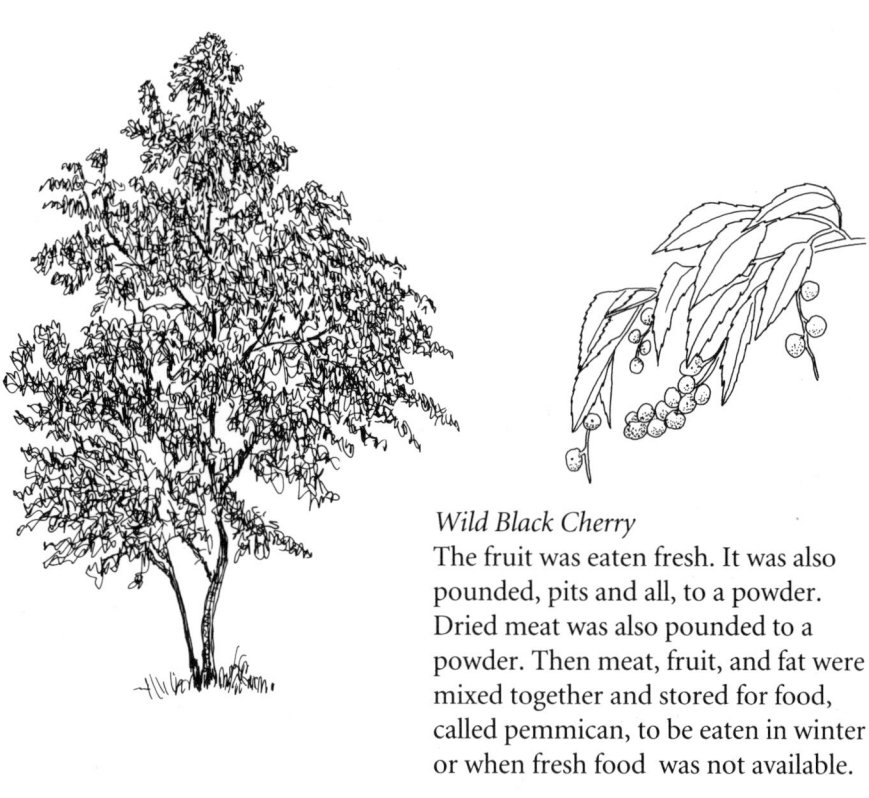

Wild Black Cherry
The fruit was eaten fresh. It was also pounded, pits and all, to a powder. Dried meat was also pounded to a powder. Then meat, fruit, and fat were mixed together and stored for food, called pemmican, to be eaten in winter or when fresh food was not available.

Relief flooded over Mi'ca. Now he could run back and feed Tangled Hoof. He walked upstream as far away from the other boys as he could. Then he ran towards the plain and began gathering arm loads of grass. He knew his way by now, but he first looked all around to be sure no one was watching him. Then he pushed through the thickets and there was Tangled Hoof who gave a little whinny of pleasure at seeing Mi'ca and the grass. Mi'ca went back several times to get more grass and then he brought some water

Mi'ca was undecided. Should he cut the vines and set Tangled Hoof free? What if he just galloped away, never to be seen again? No! Mi'ca didn't think he could stand that, especially now when Tangled Hoof seemed to be his only remaining friend. Now he could even pat the long nose and stroke the cheeks, and Tangled Hoof put his muzzle by Mi'ca's ear, letting him stroke the other cheek, and Mi'ca hugged his whole big head. He knew now that he would have to solve the problem of Tangled Hoof by himself, rather than taking it to the elders of the tribe. If he was able to resolve the problem in his own mind and do the right thing, perhaps he would be forgiven and given a man's name, as was the custom when one was ready to join the men's society. But would anyone ever accept him again in the tribe? He was almost glad now that his father was no longer alive to feel the shame of his son's disgrace.

Mi'ca felt his face burn when he remembered the black looks his Grandfather and Uncle had given him. Tangled Hoof nuzzled his shoulder and Mi'ca leaned his head against his cheek. Then, suddenly, sitting back, Mi'ca gave a low whistle and Tangled Hoof pricked up his ears. Mi'ca tried it again. This time Tangled Hoof responded with a low nicker. Mi'ca jumped up and ran out to the

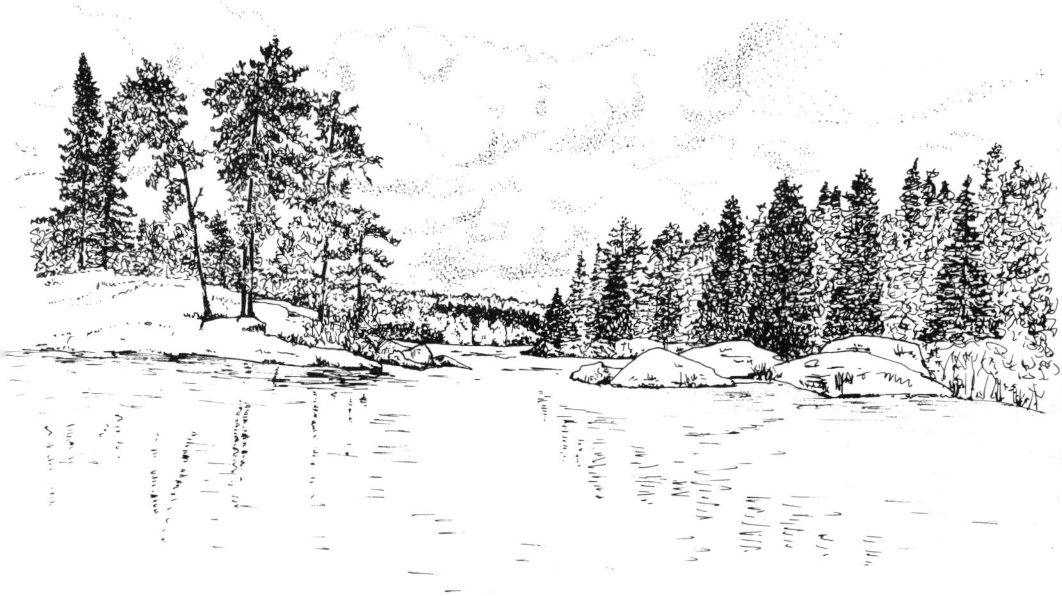

plains and gathered up more grass. Before he returned, he gave the low whistle, and then heard the nickered reply. He ran back to Tangled Hoof and gave him a tremendous hug. Then he sat beside his new friend and talked to him just as though Tangled Hoof could understand what he was saying. He told him how he would have to leave to help Ina, but promised that in the morning he would bring a knife to cut him free, and they would be able to explore the plains together. Tangled Hoof looked at him with his large brown eyes and then shook his mane. Mi'ca was sure that he had understood him and was agreeing with his plans. Mi'ca stood up and gave one last low whistle, then slipped out of the clearing and walked back to the tipi.

Willow
Wahpe popa can

7

The Chase

Mi'ca worked hard all afternoon, bringing wood for the fire and hauling water from the river and hardly saying anything. Ina made a kind of tea from the new shoots of the raspberry vines, and as they sat drinking it Mi'ca told his mother of his plan to go off by himself for a few days. She nodded her approval. He would have to prove his manhood somehow, and she knew it was important for him to leave the tribe for a while.

As soon as the stars began to fade in the early morning, Mi'ca picked up his sleeping robe, his bow and arrows in their quiver, a knife and the pair of moccasins Mahpi'ya had just made for him. He crept quietly out of the tipi and set off directly for the plain. When he got near the group of trees he gave his low whistle. There was no reply. He walked quietly closer to the trees where Tangled Hoof was and slowly pushed the bushes aside. Tangled Hoof was gone! He dropped to his knees and looked at the vine that had held Tangled Hoof, and saw that it had been chewed through.

Mi'ca sat back on his heels. He felt tears springing up in his eyes, but brushed them away and felt angry with himself. How could he hope to be a Brave if he couldn't control himself better than this? He pulled himself together and tried to give a whistle, but it didn't come out right. He stood up and looked around. Tangled Hoof might have gone down to the river to drink, and

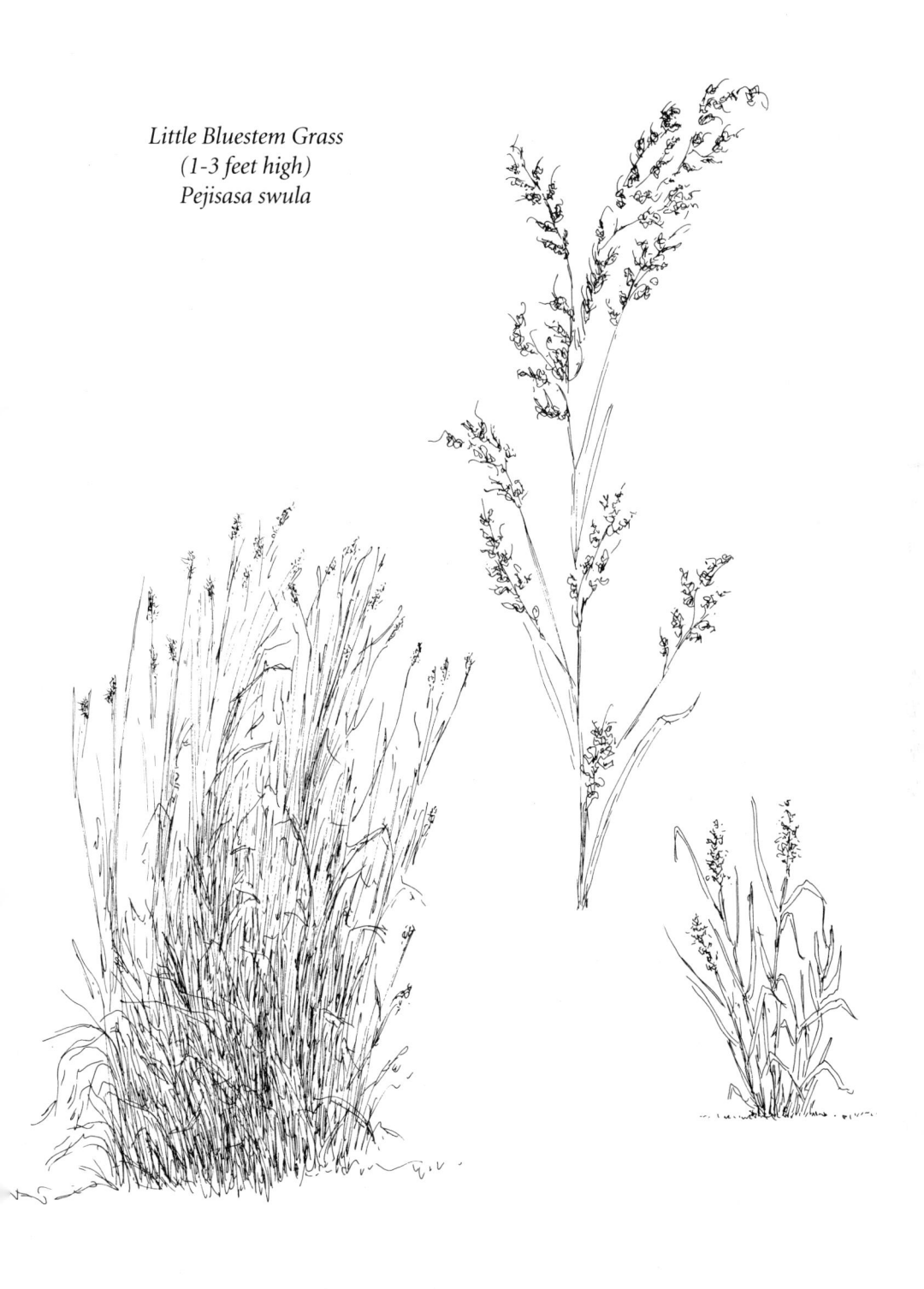

Little Bluestem Grass
(1-3 feet high)
Pejisasa swula

Mi'ca almost ran to the river bank in hopes of seeing his friend there.

But Tangled Hoof was nowhere in sight. The river bank was rather stony so that even if he had been here it would be hard to find a hoof print. Mi'ca walked upstream looking for signs, and just when he was about to give up and go back to the clearing, he noticed that the grass a bit back from the river had been cropped. There beside it was a patch of damp earth where the corner of a print could be seen. It could have been almost any hoof print and Mi'ca couldn't tell what animal had made it, but it seemed to indicate that the animal must have been moving farther upstream. Mi'ca stood up and whistled again but heard no response.

Where should he look next, along the river or on the plain? He started to move up river, then changed his mind and moved towards the plain. There were too many ferns and underbrush in the way, so he went back to the print, studied it more carefully and then looked at the surroundings. A bit farther along there was a break in the trees and brush where Tangled Hoof could have pushed through to the plain more easily. Mi'ca tried to find bits of hair from the mane or tail clinging to the bushes along the way, but saw nothing.

He soon came to another grassy place that had been cropped, and he gave a sigh of relief and continued along more rapidly. He whistled again, but only a bird answered him with a startled cry. After a while, he was out of the trees and brush and up onto the plain. The sunlight was dazzling. The sky was clear and blue and the land seemed to roll on endlessly. He took a moment to adjust his eyes to the brightness, then scanned the horizon in every direction, but there was no sign of Tangled Hoof.

Mi'ca sat down under a low willow at the edge of the plain and thought. He began to remember that one of the scouts had once told him that you could tell if a man had walked through the prairie grass by watching for the difference in the way the bent grass reflected the light. He felt sure that Tangled Hoof had come up from the river through this gap in the trees and brush. He scanned the landscape again. Was that a cropped area farther out on the plain? It was worth investigating, and when he reached the area he found it had been cropped, though some time ago since the grass stems were now dry and brittle.

There didn't seem to be any obvious trail but the grass got thinner and shorter towards the west, and if Tangled Hoof had had enough to eat he might have looked for the easiest way to walk. Farther out the longer grass looked pushed aside. Mi'ca moved quickly in that direction, scouting for the slightest trace of a trail. He kept moving farther and farther west out onto the prairie. Sometimes the grass grew tall and sometimes there were dips and hollows which made it hard to see, but now he could notice the difference in how the bent grass reflected the light and he was sure that he was on the trail of Tangled Hoof.

The plains seemed endless, and treeless too, unless there was a river valley or a lake where some trees clustered. Mi'ca walked until the sun was high overhead. He saw a large rock outcropping ahead. It was farther away than he thought, but when he did finally reach it, it offered some shade. He sat down and was about to pull out a bit of jerky until he realized that he had taken no food with him.

He leaned back against the cool rock and in a moment had dropped off to sleep. He dreamt that there were herds and herds of buffalo as far as the eye could see. The Plains were black with them. They moved slowly as though some giant wave was sweeping them along. Then suddenly one very large young bull detached himself from the moving mass and walked towards Mi'ca. He looked at Mi'ca with steady, unblinking eyes and moved closer and closer until he came directly in front of Mi'ca. There he stopped and Mi'ca could feel the hot breath blowing from his nostrils - but it was his eyes that kept him riveted. They stood face to face, neither moving a muscle.

Mi'ca woke with a start. He looked directly ahead but there was no bull before him. Neither was there a herd of buffalo to be seen, only the flat rolling prairie with its tall grasses waving with the light breeze. He closed his eyes a moment to shield them from the glare of the strong sunlight and suddenly there was the image of the bull buffalo again. Mi'ca leapt to his feet, sure now that the buffalo was his Vision-quest animal! He closed his eyes again but the vision was beginning to fade. Only the eyes of the buffalo seemed to be clear and strong and trying to send him a message. Mi'ca was sure he would recognize that buffalo the moment he saw him. No wonder his vision had not come to him while he was waiting for it in the forest or by the river cliffs; the buffalo ate the grasses of the plains and roamed free under the great open skies. It had been Mi'ca's dream all his life to live on the Plains and hunt buffalo, and now this mightiest of all buffalos was making it clear to Mi'ca that his fate was indeed entwined with the buffalo. He stood for long minute as the enormity of this revelation penetrated his consciousness. He had been alone in the wilderness; he hadn't eaten or drunk anything; and surely the intensity of the dream was overwhelming. Mi'ca was convinced that he had finally achieved his Vision-quest.

Only then did he notice that the sun had dropped farther to the west. He realized with a start that he hadn't found Tangled Hoof

Buffalo (Bison)
Tatanka

yet. He climbed to the top of the rock, but it was hard to see towards the west because the sun shone directly into his eyes. Mi'ca put his hand up to shade his eyes and then looked harder. There was something like a brown speck far to the west. There might even be some trees that way to, since the green seemed different, although the heat and sunlight made everything shimmer. Now the brown speck moved. It wasn't just another rock, it must be Tangled Hoof, it just must be! Mi'ca picked up his things and started off as quickly as possible. Now he didn't have to stop and look for signs, but he didn't want to run too fast and tire himself out because he knew it would be a very long run.

Eventually he found himself on a ridge and from there he could look down on a long, low sweep of prairie. And there, indeed, was Tangled Hoof cropping grass and moving slowly towards a group of small trees. There must be water nearby too, Mi'ca thought. He tried his low whistle, but the sound didn't carry. Mi'ca really ran now, trying to get close enough so that he could whistle again.

I mustn't be too noisy about this, he told himself, as he slowed and tried to catch his breath. He gave his whistle again, and Tangled Hoof looked up from his grazing. His ears flickered forward, but after a few moments he bent his head down and continued grazing. Mi'ca moved closer and was about to whistle again when something startled Tangled Hoof and he dashed towards the far-off trees. Mi'ca broke into a run and chased after him. After a bit Tangled Hoof slowed to an ambling walk and Mi'ca was finally able to get much closer. This time when he whistled, Tangled Hoof answered with a nicker.

Mi'ca could hardly contain his joy. He tried to move as gently as he could towards Tangled Hoof. No use in frightening him a second time, although he was sure that some other strange noise

Horse
Sun'kawakan

had frightened him earlier. Each time that Mi'ca would move closer, Tangled Hoof would step away and act wary. Mi'ca would stop and hold very still. After a long pause Mi'ca would again, very quietly, move a step closer. Tangled Hoof would graze a bit, but stepped less far away each time he moved. Finally he raised his head and looked at Mi'ca. Mi'ca began talking to Tangled Hoof, explaining how he had missed him in the morning and had spent the whole day trying to find him. Tangled Hoof shook his head up and down just as though he understood every word. By then Mi'ca was very close to Tangled Hoof so he reached out and gently patted his neck. Tangled Hoof shook his head but didn't shy away. Then side by side they began to walk towards the trees.

    The sun was dropping lower, and by the time they were among the trees an orange sunset was beginning to glow in the west. Soon they were at the edge of a small lake and Tangled Hoof put his head down and began to drink deeply. Mi'ca put his belongings on the ground and also bent down to drink, cupping water into his hands and drinking for a long time, for he was very thirsty.

    He heard a twig snap behind him and as he turned his head to look over his shoulder, he found himself surrounded by a circle of Braves. Some of the Braves held bows and arrows pointed at him. Tangled Hoof raised his head and snorted loudly. Then he stood up on his hind legs and his front legs thrashed around. He gave a loud whinny and tried to escape, but the Braves were too quick for him. One threw a rawhide rope over his head while another wound rope around his legs. A tangled hoof again! thought Mi'ca.

    He was suddenly afraid that the Braves were going to shoot their arrows at Tangled Hoof, and with a shouted "No!" he rushed over to Tangled Hoof's head and held him close in his arms. Tangled Hoof stopped thrashing about, but he was trembling.

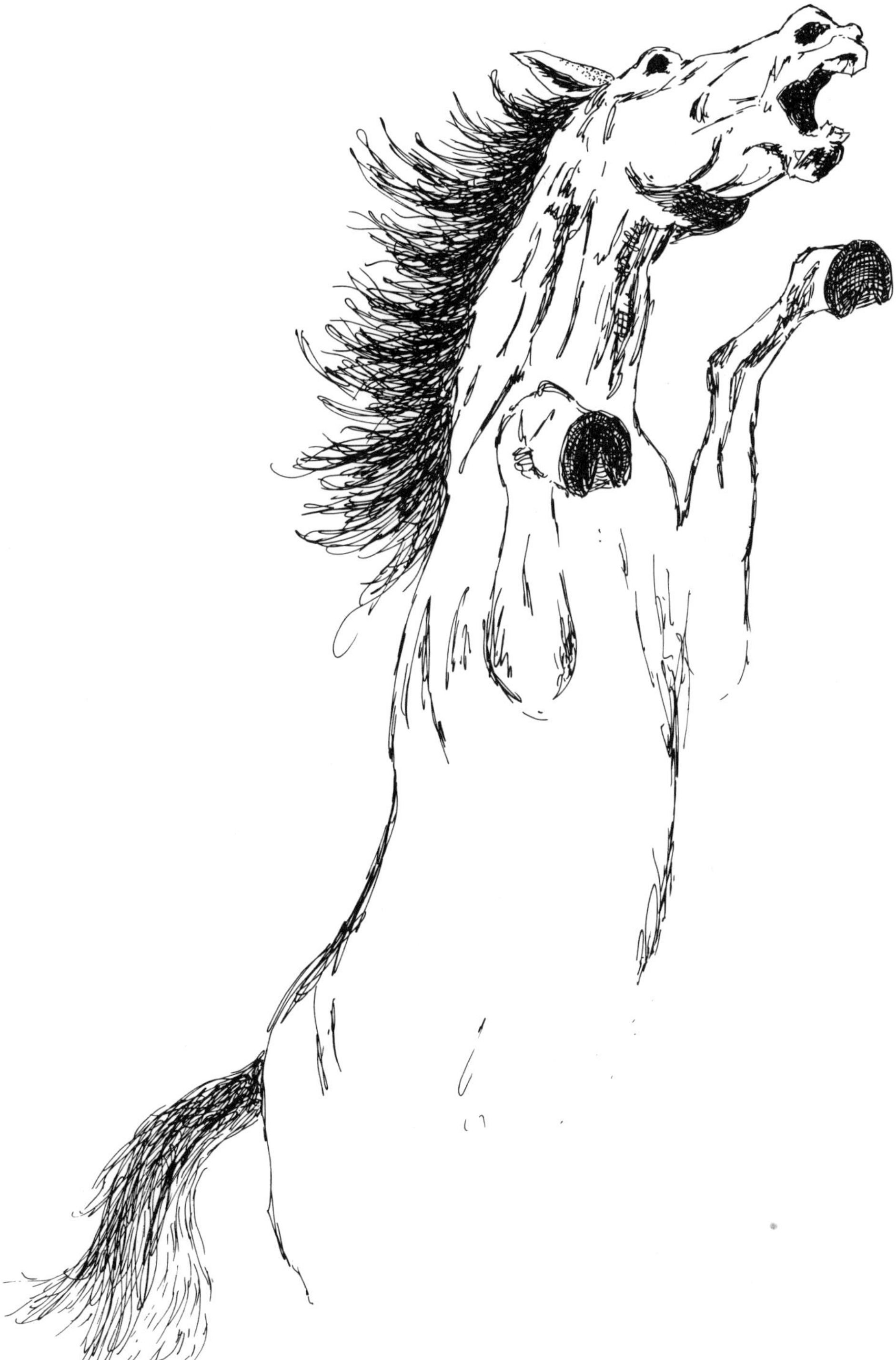

Mi'ca talked to Tangled Hoof and kept on patting him and trying to calm him down. As the animal became more quiet, Mi'ca realized that he had forgotten about his own fears and surprise.

The sun had almost set over the lake and it was hard to see the faces of the captors clearly because of the shadows, yet they certainly were not from his tribe, or even close neighbors. One of the Braves stepped forward. Mi'ca slowly straightened and released Tangled Hoof's head. He looked the Brave straight in the eye. The Brave returned his gaze and then glanced at Mi'ca's moccasins. Mi'ca glanced down at the Brave's moccasins but he didn't recognize them at all. After a few moments the Brave spoke a few words. Mi'ca felt a moment of panic when he couldn't understand what was being asked of him. But then he realized that some of the words sounded familiar. He reasoned that he was being asked his name and his tribe. One didn't usually speak one's own name, but there seemed no alternative. He swallowed hard and decided to speak in sign language

"My name is Mi'ca," he said the word aloud as he signed the word "Coyote." "I am from the Dakota tribe of the band which is called Wapeton, the Dwellers-among-the-leaves. I live in that direction." With that he pointed east and made a sign for far away, many days travel. The Brave gave a short grunt of understanding. The Braves spoke to one another for a few moments, but Mi'ca could only make out some of the words they used. Then the leader motioned Mi'ca to follow him.

Mi'ca bent down to pick up his belongings and weapons when suddenly one of the Braves grabbed him and pinned his arms back. Another Brave picked up the belongings and they gave Mi'ca a shove to get him to move to the right along the lake shore. Behind him came the Brave who had taken off the leg bindings

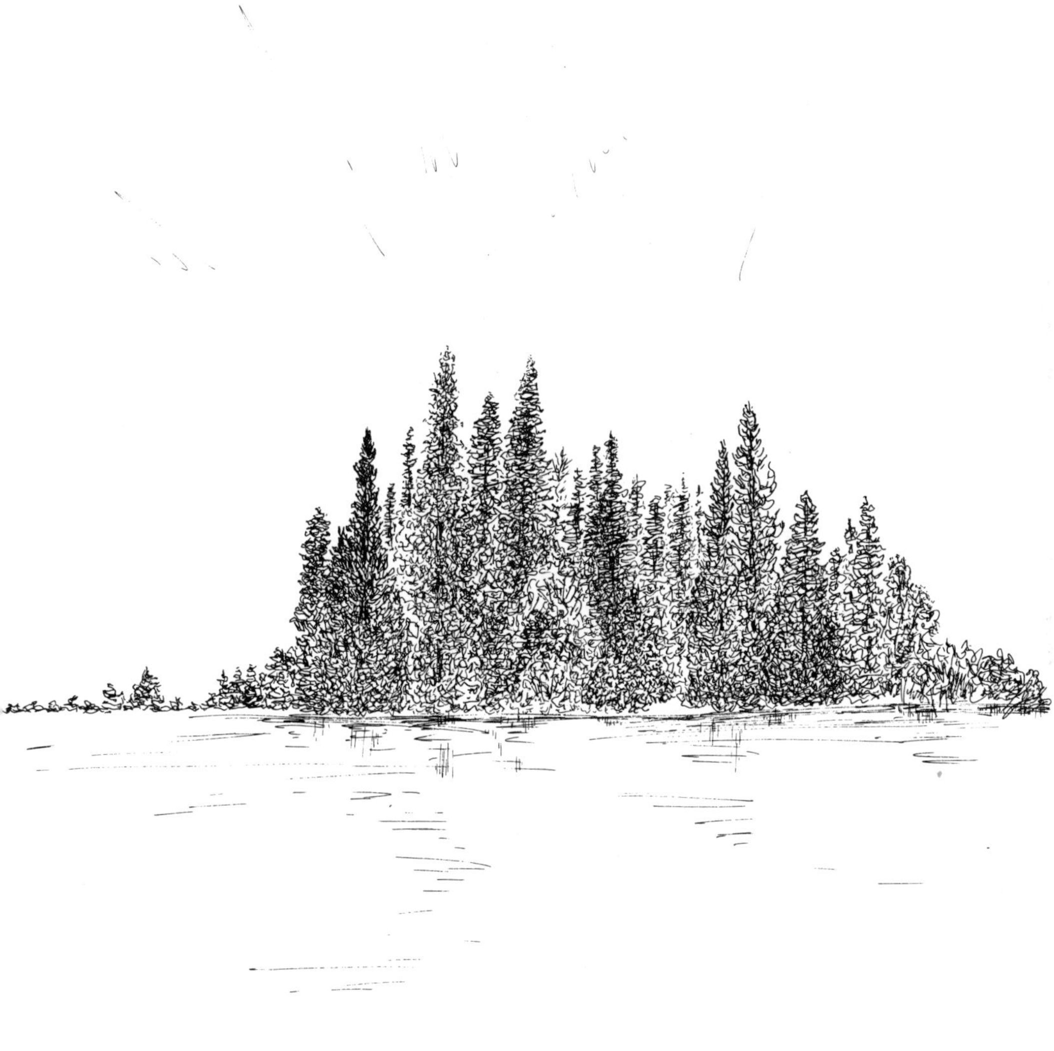

from Tangled Hoof. He now tried to lead Tangled Hoof with the ropes he had tied around his head and jaw, but Tangled Hoof snorted and thrashed about. Several Braves surrounded him and tried to get him to move forward, and all seemed to know about this kind of creature and to have even seen Tangled Hoof before. But the more they pulled the more obstinate Tangled Hoof became. And, since they seemed to be paying more attention to Tangled Hoof than they were to him, Mi'ca turned and went back to face Tangled Hoof. He began to talk to him again. This time telling him that even though they were both prisoners, perhaps it would be best for both of them if they just went along quietly with the Braves to wherever they were going to take them. Tangled Hoof quieted with the sound of Mi'ca's voice and in a few minutes Mi'ca was patting his soft muzzle and the wild look had gone out of Tangled Hoof's eyes.

Mi'ca then dared to put his hand on the rawhide rope holding Tangled Hoof's head and the Brave holding it didn't seem to object. After a moment, Mi'ca gave a gentle tug and told Tangled Hoof to come along. After a moment's hesitation he actually did take a step towards Mi'ca. Mi'ca looked over at the first Brave. Would they beat him for his daring? The first Brave stood absolutely still and looked Mi'ca in the eye again. Then with only the slightest nod of his head he indicated that it was all right. Mi'ca let out his breath and took another step forward. This time Tangled Hoof stepped more confidently and Mi'ca noticed that the other Brave had let go of the rope.

Mi'ca was leading Tangled Hoof all by himself. Very slowly he went forward along the lake shore in the direction the Brave had pointed at. There was still enough light to see where they were going, and the stony beach of the lake shore was easy to walk upon.

Speckled Butterfly
Kimimilagleglega

Prairie Smoke
Sota

Suddenly he noticed that the first Brave was in front of him and leading the way. He was taller than Tato'ka, and his movements were elastic and graceful. He must have slipped through the trees and gotten far in front before Mi'ca had noticed him. Mi'ca was immediately full of admiration for him. He was so quiet and quick and steady. Yes, those were qualities his uncle had often talked about. Mi'ca had never been quite sure just what they meant, but he thought he was beginning to understand it now. The Brave had looked at Mi'ca with steady eyes. He had made up his mind to trust Mi'ca with Tangled Hoof, and had stood there absolutely still as Mi'ca had quieted the frightened beast. And now he had appeared before him on the shore without making a sound. The group moved silently forward with the other Braves following behind Mi'ca and Tangled Hoof. Ahead Mi'ca saw the light of a campfire.

As they came close to it Tangled Hoof began to move quickly and gave out a neigh. There were a few answering snorts. Mi'ca grabbed the rein tighter, and as they came near the campfire, Mi'ca saw a whole group of beasts just like Tangled Hoof. But they were not all of a dark brown color: some were black, some were light tan, and some were a mixture of black and white as though they had been painted in large splashes. Tangled Hoof seemed to know them and even trot towards them with a light step.

Compass Plant
Cansinsinla

Used to find direction since the lower leaves always face north.

8

The Great Plains

Mi'ca's eyes opened wide with wonder at the sight of all these animals. The first Brave quietly took the lead from Mi'ca's hands, walked Tangled Hoof over to the other animals and tied his legs together so that he could not stray. Mi'ca then noticed that the other animals also had their legs tied. In the flickering campfire light Mi'ca couldn't tell how many of these animals there were, perhaps twelve.

The first Brave came over to him, said something, pointing towards the fire and told him in sign language to sit down. The other Braves were already seated. Clearly, they were going to decide his fate. Would they kill him? He gave a little shudder of fear. Maybe they would just make him their slave. Who were these Braves, anyhow? He couldn't remember ever seeing anyone like them or hearing the elders speak of such people, and, yet, when they spoke he felt that he could understand some of their words. It was good that his uncle had taught him sign language, because he knew enough to help him out now that he needed it.

They brought out his belongings and looked at his bow and arrows closely. They handled the things carefully and passed them from hand to hand. Mi'ca was proud of them. He pointed to himself and then held his hand out and said, "Tunkan'sidan." To try to tell the Braves that both he and his grandfather had worked

Coyote
Mi'caksica

on them together. The Braves turned toward each other and said, "Tunka'sila?" And although they pronounced the word differently, it was clear that they had understood him. The first Brave, who was named Wa'o'ka, marksman, raised his arm and swept it around in a circle to indicate all those who sat around the campfire and said, "Teton, Lakota." The Braves spoke a few words among themselves, glancing at Mi'ca. Then they put the bow and arrows back in the quiver and examined the shape and design on Mi'ca's moccasins. Mi'ca thought of his mother and sister and he suddenly felt homesick.

No one would miss him and come looking for him now, since he had told his mother that he wanted to travel alone. They would be even less inclined to seek him out after his disgrace. But then he held up his head. He hadn't failed in the end. He had fasted, almost by accident since he had forgotten to bring food. The image of the great bull buffalo was still strongly in his mind, and almost without thinking he blurted out that he had dreamed of his Vision-quest animal. The Braves who had been reserved and almost hostile, drew back. What was that Mi'ca had just told them? Wa'o'ka said something to Mi'ca in a commanding tone. Mi'ca put his shoulders back and said, "Ta'tan'ka" and, by curving his index fingers over his head like buffalo horns, gave the sign for buffalo. Then he threw his arms wide to indicate a huge beast. The Braves seemed to be all talking at once as they began to understand what Mi'ca had said about his Vision-quest. He felt their hostility ebb and the tension eased. A boy on a Vision-quest was quite a different matter from a boy who seemed to be stealing Tangled Hoof.

Wa'o'ka stood up and walked over to a cooking pouch, helping himself to some stew. The other Braves followed. When they had finished eating Wa'o'ka signalled for Mi'ca to come over and eat.

Meadowlark
Jia lepa

A boy of about Mi'ca's age was tending the fire and their eyes met briefly as he handed Mi'ca a horn spoon full of meat. Mi'ca was both very hungry and terribly tired. When he had finished eating Wa'o'ka handed him his sleeping robe and then tied a thong to Mi'ca's leg. The other end he tied to his own leg so that if Mi'ca tried to escape in the night the tug would waken him.

Mi'ca hadn't thought much about escaping, but for tonight it was certainly out of the question. He didn't know where these Braves had come from, but they hadn't been cruel to him. They might even be related to his tribe since they called themselves Teton Lakotah, which sounded a bit like Wapeton Dakota, and he could understand quite a lot of what they said. As he wrapped himself up in his robe he wondered if his own tribe would allow him to return. Even his friends had ridiculed him. Would they forgive him now that the buffalo had appeared to him? Mi'ca felt unsure that they would ever forget and forgive him. Then there was Tangled Hoof. He felt strongly that he couldn't leave him. But where were they taking him and all those other animals like him?

When Mi'ca awoke the sky was clear and bright and the dawn light was showing in the east. Where the air had been so still and silent a moment before, it was now filled with sound. Birds called and Mi'ca recognized the meadowlark. His people called it the bird of promise, for it's song seemed to say "I will whistle for the buffalo to come to you. Mi'ca sent a silent wish to the bird that he might see all the buffalo the bird promised to send with his song.
 The Brave awoke and untied Mi'ca. They took the animals to the lake to drink and then staked them in a grassy spot so they could graze. The Braves then went to bathe. Mi'ca was glad he was allowed to bathe and swim after the long run of the previous day. The lake water was pleasant, but quiet and warm and very unlike the river.

Beaver
Cha'pa

Mi'ca swam a short distance with his overhead racing strokes, but then remembered to paddle like a beaver, and with a push went under and moved along quickly before he had to surface again for air. After that he moved back to the shore with his nose just above the water, certainly easier to do on a calm lake than a river. As he reached the shore he noticed that several Braves were watching him. Their faces were impassive, but he thought he caught a look of approval in their eyes.

The morning meal was soon eaten and again Mi'ca was only permitted to eat when the others had finished. The campfire was put out and the campsite carefully arranged to make it appear as though no one had ever been there. Old leaves were scattered around the sleeping places and all footprints smoothed away, much of the work was done by the young boy Mi'ca had sen the night before. In his own tribe, Mi'ca knew, it was a great honor for a young boy to be chosen to accompany a band of Braves and to be of help to them.

They were ready to leave. The animals were gathered and pulled by their leads. But Tangled Hoof balked. First he pulled his head back with a snort and then started pulling with his whole body and thrashing with his head to loosen the thongs. Mi'ca gave his low whistle and took a step towards him, but then he remembered where he was and turned to look at Wa'o'ka. Wa'o'ka gave the slight nod of the head. Yes, it was alright for him to quiet the animal and lead him. Mi'ca stood by his friend and talked to him about the lake and what it felt like to swim in there, and little by little Tangled Hoof calmed down and finally nuzzled Mi'ca's shoulder.

Mi'ca took a few steps and Tangled Hoof quieted and came along. They followed the trail made by the other Braves who had gone ahead with their animals, though two Braves stayed behind

*Prairie
Tiiheyapaya*

him. One stayed close, to watch both him and Tangled Hoof, Mi'ca was sure. The other stayed much farther behind, acting as a rear scout and obliterating any signs that the party had passed there.

They were clearly moving through territory which was not theirs and they didn't want to be discovered by scouts of other tribes. Now they certainly wouldn't let Mi'ca go since he might reveal where they were. If Mi'ca tried to escape and they caught him, they would certainly kill him. He patted Tangled Hoof on the nose and whispered to him to please behave so they could travel with the Braves and not get into trouble.

Now they began moving quickly westward across the plain. These were indeed the Great Plains that Mi'ca had always dreamed about. The land was covered with high grass that waved and swayed with each breeze. It seemed to stretch on endlessly, flat to the horizon and flat from North to South. After a very long time they came to a natural depression in the prairie and they posted a scout at the rim as the rest of the party went down into it. There they rested and the animals grazed until they were ready to move again. They continued until they came to a small brook at evening-time where they made camp for the night.

It was much like the night before, with a warming fire and the animals hobbled nearby, except that in the morning there was no lake. One could only splash a bit of water on one's face and body and bring the animals down to drink from the tiny stream. When they started again it was clear that it was Mi'ca's duty to take care of Tangled Hoof. When the other Braves tried to lead him he only became balky and stubborn, but he followed Mi'ca with no trouble. Mi'ca couldn't have been happier. When he walked along leading Tangled Hoof he was only aware of the bright warm sun and the enormity of the space of the Plains. There were no trees or hills to

Jack Rabbit
Mastinska

Calling rabbits by
making a kissing sound
by holding the fingers
to the lips.

soften the wind so that one felt its constant tension in the air. It made Mi'ca's step buoyant.

Each day a few Braves would hunt for fresh meat. Usually they brought back rabbits or Jack rabbits for they were everywhere on the Plains, and could be brought down with a blunt pointed arrow or even just with the shaft of an arrow sharpened to a point. One of the Braves was very clever at attracting the rabbits by making a kissing sound by pressing his fingers against his lips. As the rabbits came to investigate he would hurl a rock at them and was able to hit them almost every time. This had earned him the name Running Rabbit. Mi'ca tried to imitate the way he hurled the rocks, but Tangled Hoof shied when the rocks whistled past his ears, so he could only practice when the animals were grazing.

One day a scout who was on the crest of a hill held up his hand with his first finger crooked. He had sighted Pronghorns. The Braves halted and quietly hobbled the animals. Several of the Braves left the group to join the scout. After a while they came back with several Pronghorns slung over their backs. They were laughing and joking among themselves as they dropped the game down beside the fire. They had tricked the Pronghorns by creeping quietly through the tall grass until they were close to the herd. Then they put a piece of brightly painted robe on a stick and slowly waved it above the top of the grass. One by one the curious Pronghorns stepped cautiously through the grass to investigate. When one came close enough, a Brave could raise up on one knee and send an arrow into it. Mi'ca had never tasted Pronghorn meat before, but he liked it so much that he was glad that it lasted them several days. He noticed that the Braves scraped the skins very carefully before they rolled them up and saved them to bring back to their camp. He could see that the skin would make very soft clothing.

Pronghorn Antelope
Tato'kadan

Sign language sign for pronghorn.

Although they saw several more great herds of Pronghorns, they were always too far away to hunt. Sometimes they saw only a great cloud of dust racing along near the horizon but moving so quickly that the scouts only had to glance at it to know that they were Pronghorn.

Mi'ca felt so excited about this travel across the Plains that he found it hard not to break into a run while leading Tangled Hoof. He paid special attention to how the scouts tracked game on the Plains. It was quiet different from stalking game in the woods. One of the scouts would crawl on his belly to the top of a grassy ridge and then very carefully pull up a bunch of grass by the roots and look under the roots to see what was before him. The game never seemed to be surprised that the tops of the waving grass suddenly moved upward before their eyes! The scout could always use hand signals to tell the others below what he had found. The scouts were even more careful to keep down wind of the animals, since the prairie wind blew so strongly. Man scents alerted all the animals and even the slightest whiff was enough to stampede any herd. Sometimes the scouts draped a skin over themselves and scattered dirt over it to camouflage themselves and disguise the scent further. By remaining quiet they looked almost like a boulder. Other times they covered themselves with grass and moved silently along when the tall prairie grass leaned and doubled before the wind. But one thing was common to both woodland and prairie scouts - the way they moved. They almost glided when they were near game and so quietly that they blended with the land.

At night, when the animals had been picketed with a rope long enough for them to move about and graze, and the camp fire had burned itself out, Mi'ca would lie on his buffalo robe and watch the stars. The night-shadowed prairie was a thing of wonder to

Indian Grass
Pejisasa inkpa jiji

him. Nothing he had known could equal the loneliness and solitude of this stillness. Far off he could hear a wolf howl, breaking the spell and making the voice of solitude audible. Mi'ca sighed with utter contentment and dropped off to sleep.

During the next days a few of the Braves tried to speak to Mi'ca. It was halting at first, but with sign language and pointing at objects to learn their names, Mi'ca was beginning to understand what they were saying. The other boys name, he found out, was Toka'la, Kit Fox. They usually were sent out together to collect twigs or buffalo chips for the fire, but somehow they felt a bit shy about speaking freely to one another.

The animals always needed to graze and drink water, so the progress across the plains was rather slow. One day they came to a large river and followed its course. There were trees and shrubs along the banks and it was a pleasant change. But towards evening the sky clouded over and a heavy storm threatened. The Braves tethered the animals close together and quickly gathered underbrush to make a crude shelter for themselves. Then Wa'o'ka called the Braves together and they sat in a circle and sought to propitiate the mysteries that control the winds. Wa'o'ka filled his pipe and extended it to the West, where lightening was already flickering. In the West was the Nation of Thunder where the Wing Flappers, who first existed, dwelt. He offered the pipe to the remaining three Winds, the Sky and the Earth, and when that was done he lit the pipe and passed it around the circle. Lightening split the darkened sky, followed by thunder which broke with a tremendous crash just above them. The animals neighed and strained at their thongs. Mi'ca and Toka'la ran to hold and quiet them as the Braves passed the pipe around once more to appease the forces of nature, Wakan, which no man can understand.

Kit Fox
Toka'la

The rain pelted down and for a few minutes turned into sharp driving hail stones.

When the brief, violent storm had passed, they pulled down the brush shelter and used the dry leaves under it to start a fire. The heavy cottonwood trees near the river had protected them from the worst of the rain, but only a short distance away they saw one tree which had been split down the middle by a lightening bolt. The Braves murmured about the powers of Wakan and decided this was a sign for them to leave the river the next morning and strike out again across the Plain.

The animals were tethered close to the campfire that night and as soon as the sky whitened with the first pale light of day, the Braves were up and ready to leave. Wa'o'ka stood beside Mi'ca and raised his hand toward the South. There was a black moving mass which stretched on and on, and Mi'ca gasped when he realized it was a huge herd of buffalo. Wa'o'ka looked uneasy and spoke a few words to the other Braves which Mi'ca didn't quite catch. The band started off westward again and moved as quickly and as noiselessly as possible towards a large stand of trees on the horizon. As soon as they reached them, scouts were sent out towards the buffalo herds. No fire was made and the remaining Braves patted the animals to keep them quiet, and then laid down to rest. By nightfall the scouts returned and told of seeing a large group of people following the herd, with hunters shooting the animals and the women cutting up the meat. One scout was sure that he had been seen and it would not be long before scouts of the buffalo hunters would be coming after him. He was quite nervous, fearing that this large band would chase them down.

Wa'o'ka held up his hand, looked very stern and said, "You, Hawk Tail, absolutely close your mouth. We will leave this spot

Buffalo Grass
Sipawicakase

immediately and travel west as quickly as we can." There were a few worried words and then everyone gathered their belongings and the group moved out of the trees and across the prairie.

It was very dark but the sure-footed Braves had no trouble running along silently. Mi'ca had not grown up on the Plains and stumbled occasionally. Then he felt a guiding hand on his elbow: it was Toka'la. The two ran along silently. The coyotes and the wolves howled occasionally and at one point they clearly heard the shouting and yelling from the grove of trees they had left. Their enemies had found them gone and now the Braves and animals quickened their pace. With the dawn they turned towards a stream bed with a small creek and a few scattered trees. The animals were tethered and the Braves felt that it was safe to build a small fire. They felt sure that the pursuing tribe would have returned to the buffalo kill rather than continue to chase them. Some meat was roasted over the fire and as soon as they had eaten, two guards were posted and the rest wrapped their sleeping robes around themselves and slept. In the early afternoon the guard was changed and a hunter followed the creek downstream to look for game for the camp. He coaxed a deer out by sucking on a leaf folded between his lips. The sound it made was like the whimper of a fawn, and deer showed her head to investigate. The hunter shot his arrow and was able to bring fresh meat to the camp. After they had eaten, they began their second night of travel across the Plain. When half the night was gone, Wa'o'ka gathered them around and asked if they felt as he did that they could now stop and sleep. Everyone agreed, and the tired men and animals bedded down for what was left of the night.

At dawn a brave named Spotted Eagle woke the camp with loud singing and dancing. When everyone was fully awake he shouted that a raven had flown out of the West and come directly

Raven
Kangi tanka

Wingspread
four feet

overhead. He had then flown twice around in a circle before flying off to the West again. He felt that the raven was giving them a message that the camp of their people was close. The Braves were very cheerful after that and after two more days of travel were on their own hunting territory.

*Camp
Agliti*

9

Lakota Captive

In the last day of their travel they were sighted by their own scouts, and news of their arrival spread quickly. As they came closer to the encampment, Mi'ca saw that the tipis had been placed in a huge circle, with more tipis than he had ever seen together. The Braves came into the center of the circle where the great Council Tipi stood. Everyone had come out of their tipis to watch, and it was clear from the surprised look on the faces of the people and their cries of "Ho!" that they, too, had never seen the strange animals which the Braves brought with them.

The Chief stood in the center to welcome the group back, and motioned that the animals be tethered to one side. Then he spoke to the people gathered about. "This evening there must be a great Council Fire where the Braves will speak and tell of their adventures and how they were able to bring these wonderful animals to our tribe."

Mi'ca stood tall and quiet behind the group of Braves, but once the animals had been led away he found some of the children staring at him and began to feel self-conscious. He wondered again what they would do with him. He was almost certain now that they had no intention of killing him, and he gave an audible sigh of relief. They would probably keep him here as a captive, but if he could still take care of Tangled Hoof, perhaps it wouldn't be so

Kimimila zi
Yellow Butterfly

Kimimila ska
White butterfly

Also the name for small white moths that flew around flame. They were praised as "fearless as a white moth."

Blue-eyed Grass

bad. Travelling across the prairie had been exciting and he hoped there would be other travels, and maybe he could even hunt buffalo. Suddenly he noticed that it had grown very silent around him and everyone was looking at him. He tried to look confident and not move a muscle.

At last the Chief spoke to Wa'o'ka and motioned in sign language that Mi'ca should follow Wa'o'ka to his tipi. Mi'ca was pleased, and tried to indicate it with his eyes, though it wouldn't do to smile now. He followed Wa'o'ka across the clearing to a tipi much larger than his old home. He was shown a place to put down his robe. Wa'o'ka then motioned for him to follow him out. They went a fair distance down a slope to a stream where they could wash the dust and dirt of travel off their bodies. Mi'ca and Wa'o'ka lingered a long time in the stream, a narrower and slower flowing river than Mi'ca was used to, but the water was good and clear.

When they got back to the tipi a stew of fresh buffalo meat with turnips was ready for them. Mi'ca again had to wait until Wa'o'ka was finished eating, but then he could have as much as he liked, and it was almost as if he were at home. Wa'o'ka's wife, Lark Woman, was much younger than his own mother, but she had learned how to cook well, and her eyes looked at Mi'ca with kindness.

After eating he followed Wa'o'ka to the council fire. The men of the tribe sat in a circle and passed the pipe around. The women and children were behind them. The drum was sounding a slow steady rhythm but when the Chief rose to his feet to speak there was one loud drum beat and the drumming stopped. The Chief began by welcoming back his Braves after a long and difficult journey, and praising their valor and cunning in obtaining the animals they had sought. Then he sat, and the Braves spoke of

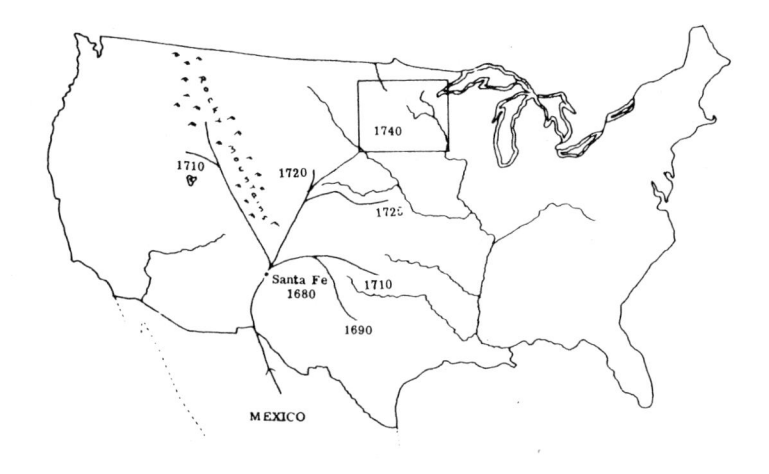

Dispersion of Horses from Santa Fe by date

Horses were brought to America by the Spanish Conquitadors. By 1600 they were brought from Mexico as far north as Santa Fe. The enslaved Pueblo Indians formed an alliance with the Apache and Navajo Indians and revolted in 1680. The Spaniards abandoned the Rancheros and fled. Thousands of horses were set free by the Indians.

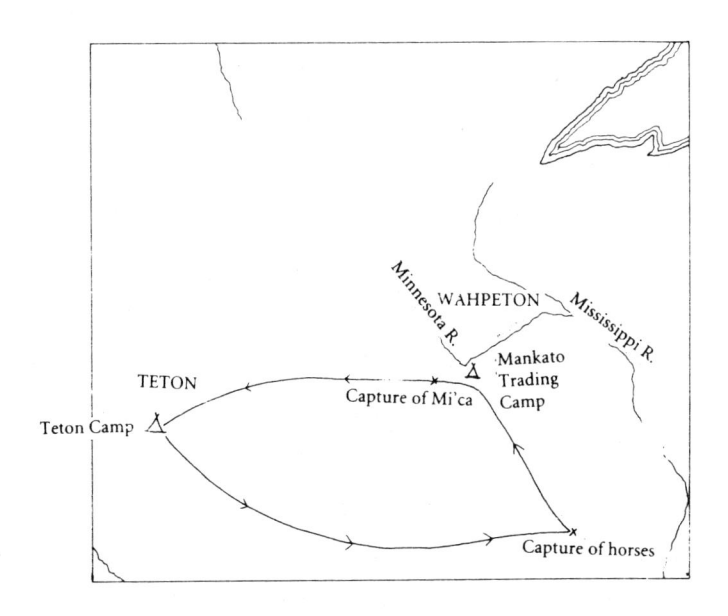

Route of the Teton Braves

their adventures. One got up and told of the journey towards the southeast where they had first encountered hostile tribes and had had to fight before they could continue their journey.

Another described the first sightings of the strange animals, but they saw only a few of them with many warriors guarding them. The Braves had watched for a long time and had been surprised to see some of the warriors sitting on the backs of these animals, seemingly carried with great ease and running as swift as the wind, faster even than a buffalo. The Braves then wanted some of these animals more than ever. But it was not possible for the Braves to capture these animals. As they continued their travels they began to see more and more of the animals, and they had circled the area for many days until they found the least guarded animals. Those they had captured and brought back.

Wa'o'ka picked up the story and told how they had crept up in the night, grabbed the leads on the horses's heads and had pulled the animals along behind them. They had killed two guards in the process, but it was done quietly so the camp was not aroused. Another Brave stood and told how they had moved north with the animals, mostly at night to avoid detection. They had had much trouble with one of the animals, a brown one with white bands on his legs. He was always unruly and breaking away, but he was such a fine animal that they felt it worth the effort to keep him with the band. Then one day he broke completely free and galloped off and no one could catch him. He ran north along a big river and though they searched for three days, they could not find him. On the fourth day they had turned west and camped by the shore of a small lake. There they had finally seen the wild one together with this one, and he pointed at Mi'ca. He, Mi'ca, was trying to call the wild one to him, so they watched and waited. But just then one of

*Hawk
Cetan*

the Braves had sneezed and the animal had dashed away again. But eventually, this one and the wild animal had come down together to the lake shore to drink and the Braves had surrounded them and captured both of them by surprise. Finally another Brave told the story of the return journey.

The Chief stood again and praised the Braves. They had done well, surviving a long and difficult journey, fighting bravely when necessary, and bringing the wonderful animals back to the tribe. Now anyone at the council fire could speak up and tell what they knew of these strange new beasts.

An old man stood up and said that he had heard a story many years before, that long, long ago before his grandfather's grandfather had been born, men came to our land in large boats from the direction of the rising sun. They were very odd men with shiny clothes of hard metal, and with much hair on their faces and a skin that was of a pale color. Worse they had sticks of metal which belched fire, and when they pointed them at a person, that person fell dead. With these people came these new strange animals which could carry things on their backs as well as carry men. Their name for them was cabayo, horse.

The old man sat down and a woman then stood up. She had been captured as a child and brought to the tribe. Her own people, who lived far to the southwest, were pueblo. Long, long ago, she began, before her Grandfather's Grandfather had lived, these men who had been spoken of just now, came to her tribe and made everyone a slave to them. They called themselves Spaniards. They treated the Pueblo people cruelly, and after many years of enslavement the Pueblo people rose up in revolt, burned the villages and killed many of their oppressors, and then they set free all of the animals. Some of the Pueblo people knew how to take care of them

Aster
Wahca zi waste

Young leaves
eaten as greens.

and how to ride on their backs and so they took the horses with them. While many other people just ran away and hid and many, many animals were set free to run away into the wild. She had heard that there were still large groups of these animals roaming wild across the land, but this was something she had never seen but only heard about in tales.

Another Brave stood up and said that he, too, had heard about a strange beast that tribes far to the south of our own Sioux Nation had, and they were called Big Dog. Everyone knew that dogs were intelligent and that they would work for a man. These new animals were much bigger than dogs, and if they could be used as helpers, he wanted to call the new animal Big Dog. Another Brave stood up and said that he had heard them called Mystery Dogs, or Special Dogs, Sun'kawakan.

There was much talk as everyone exclaimed their surprise at the stories they had heard. When the talking quieted, the Chief raised his hand, "It has been decided that these new animals should be called Sun'kawakan. Mi'ca hadn't understood all that had been said, especially what the Pueblo woman had talked about, but he had understood a great deal. The Chief again raised his hand. There was now another decision to be made: who would look after the Sun'kwakan and who would try sitting on their backs?

Wa'o'ka stood up and said he liked the animals and at least for now he was willing to stake them near his tipi and see that they were taken care of. He had brought back the captive and would have him help with the task. As for riding on their backs, perhaps the Braves who had accompanied him on the raid should be the first to try, since they knew the animals best. Wa'o'ka pointed to Mi'ca and said that perhaps he, too, should try to sit on their backs

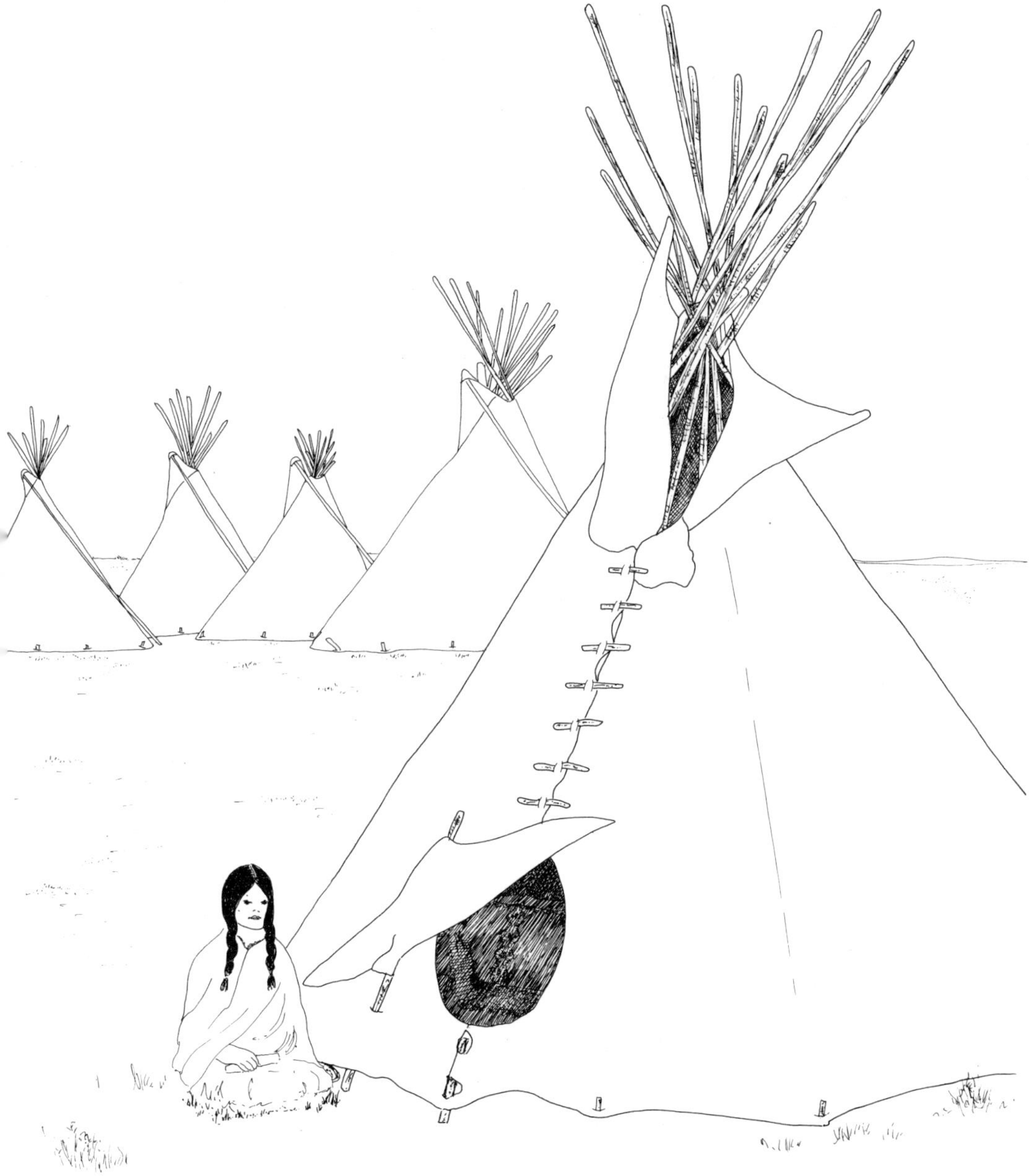

since he had been able to quiet the animals when they had been difficult to handle.

Mi'ca felt all the eyes turn to look at him again. He was tremendously excited but knew that he would be expected to respond calmly and quietly to this news. Nevertheless, his eyes were shining. This was obviously a great test to see if he would respond correctly and even the small children of the Teton didn't make any noise as they stared at him. After a seemingly endless time the Chief spoke. Yes, he agreed with Wa'o'ka. If the Braves had not felt it necessary to kill Mi'ca when they first found him, or along the trail back, and they had been satisfied with his help with the Sun'kawakan, then Wa'o'ka could continue to use him and perhaps educate him in the ways of the Teton Sioux.

Mi'ca could barely contain himself. Think of sitting on Tangled Hoof's back! He had seen how fast Tangled Hoof could run, and if he could sit on his back when Tangled Hoof ran like that, it would be like flying on the wind.

Everyone was now talking again and Mi'ca dared to turn towards Wa'o'ka. Wa'o'ka had been watching Mi'ca carefully and was clearly pleased with his deportment. There was the slightest smile on his lips now as their eyes met. Everyone was walking about now. The women urging the small children to go to bed, and the boys of his age forming a group some distance away from the fire. The boys talked and laughed and Mi'ca realized with a sinking heart that he wasn't part of a play group any longer. As a captive he now had to work and be helpful, not play and have fun. Wa'o'ka touched his shoulder and indicated the direction to his tipi.

Butterfly
Kimimila

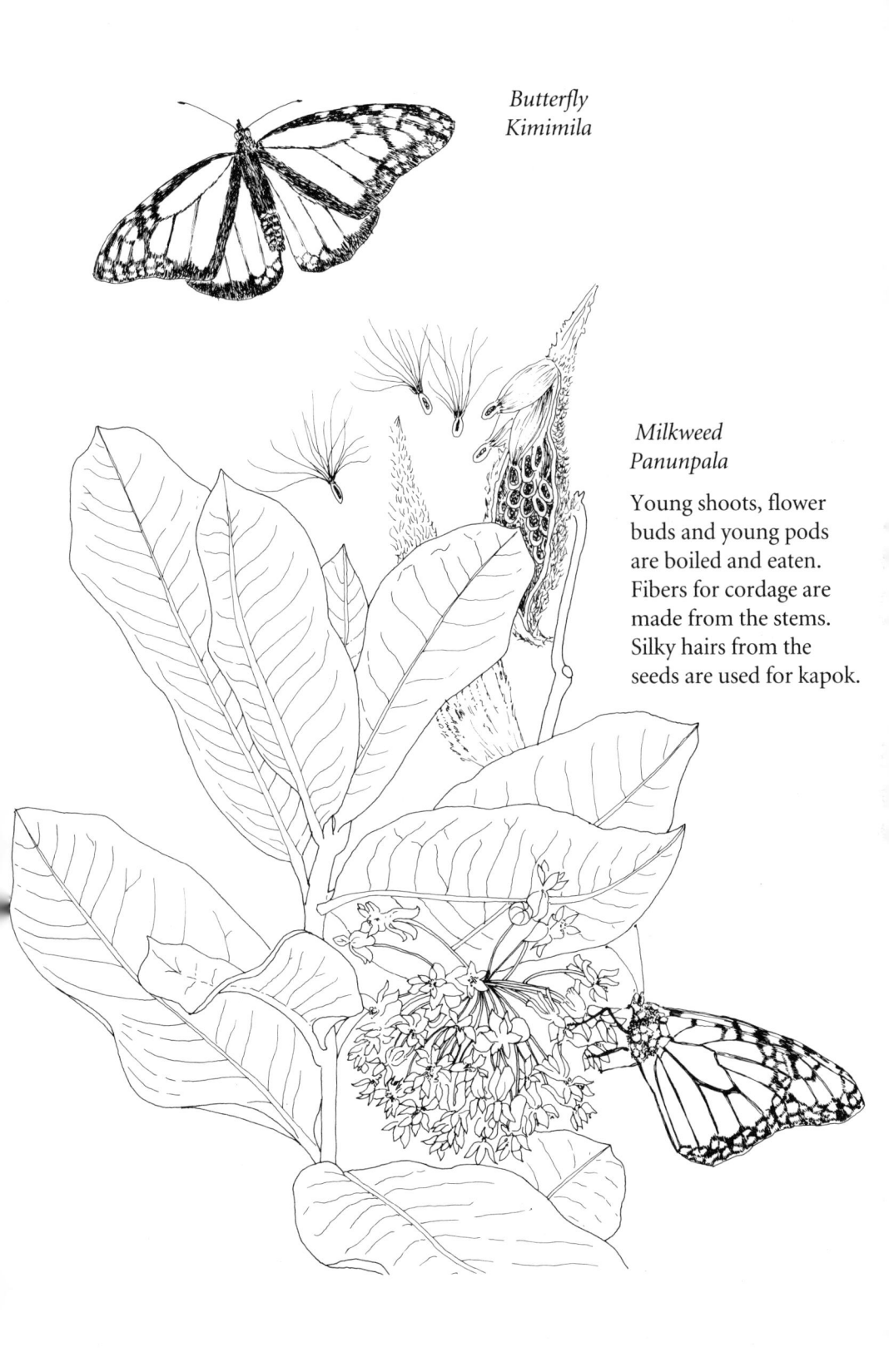

Milkweed
Panunpala

Young shoots, flower buds and young pods are boiled and eaten. Fibers for cordage are made from the stems. Silky hairs from the seeds are used for kapok.

10

Sun'kawakan

The next morning, after they had bathed in the stream and eaten, Mi'ca and Wa'o'ka walked over to the Sun'kawakan. The other Braves also came and they stood together discussing what they should do. Finally, Running Rabbit said he thought the animals would like it better if they were not tied down all the time, but could move about and lie where they liked as dogs did, but keeping them from running away was a problem. Poles like the ones that held up the tipi were too scarce on the open prairie, so it would be hard to build a fence with poles. But underbrush of old dead bushes piled up might work. They walked beside the stream to see what they could find and began gathering the brush and carrying it up to where the animals were tied. One of the Braves noticed the boys playing not far off and shouted for them to come and help. Toka'la was one of the boys who came, and he and Mi'ca smiled briefly at each other.

    Everyone worked hard and piled the brush in a big circle around the animals. It looked safe enough and they let loose one of the small quiet mares. She moved around but didn't try to jump over the brush or break down the barrier and they all felt relieved. All the boys except Toka'la went back to their games. The Braves, Mi'ca and Toka'la then brought all the Sun'kawakan down to the stream to drink and then all except the small mare were taken to

Cottontail Rabbit
Mastinsapa

the plains to graze. Wa'o'ka, Running Rabbit, Mi'ca and Toka'la took her back to the brush circle. When the brush circle was closed, Mi'ca stood by the head of the animal and held the rawhide rope, which had been tied around her lower jaw.

Running Rabbit put his arms across the back of the mare, and with Wa'o'ka's help, slid slowly and calmly up onto the mare's back. The mare shied, surprising Mi'ca, who let go of the bridle. The animal jumped away, and Running Rabbit grabbed for the mane and clung to it while the others ran after the man and animal. In a few minutes everything was under control again and the mare quieted down and walked rather than jumped. Mi'ca and Toka'la began to walk on either side of the animal's head, around and around the circle. They continued in this fashion for quite a while until Running Rabbit began to feel secure. They were abruptly interrupted by one of the Braves who ran up, shouting for Mi'ca to come quickly and help with the wild one.

Mi'ca pushed the brush aside, and, closing the gap behind him, ran after the Brave. As he reached the group of Braves and animals, there was Tangled Hoof, rearing and snorting. Mi'ca gave his low whistle and Tangled Hoof paused long enough to hear him, but a moment later he was thrashing around again. Tangled Hoof had behaved well on the trail, but then Mi'ca had been beside him day and night. Now, back in camp, they had been separated and Tangled Hoof was letting everyone know he didn't like it. Mi'ca ran to his friend, whistled again and began to talk to him. He told him about the meeting last night and how the young mare was letting herself be ridden and how well she was behaving compared to Tangled Hoof. As he spoke, Tangled Hoof finally quieted and Mi'ca noticed that the other Braves had been listening hard to understand what he was saying about the mare. So he said

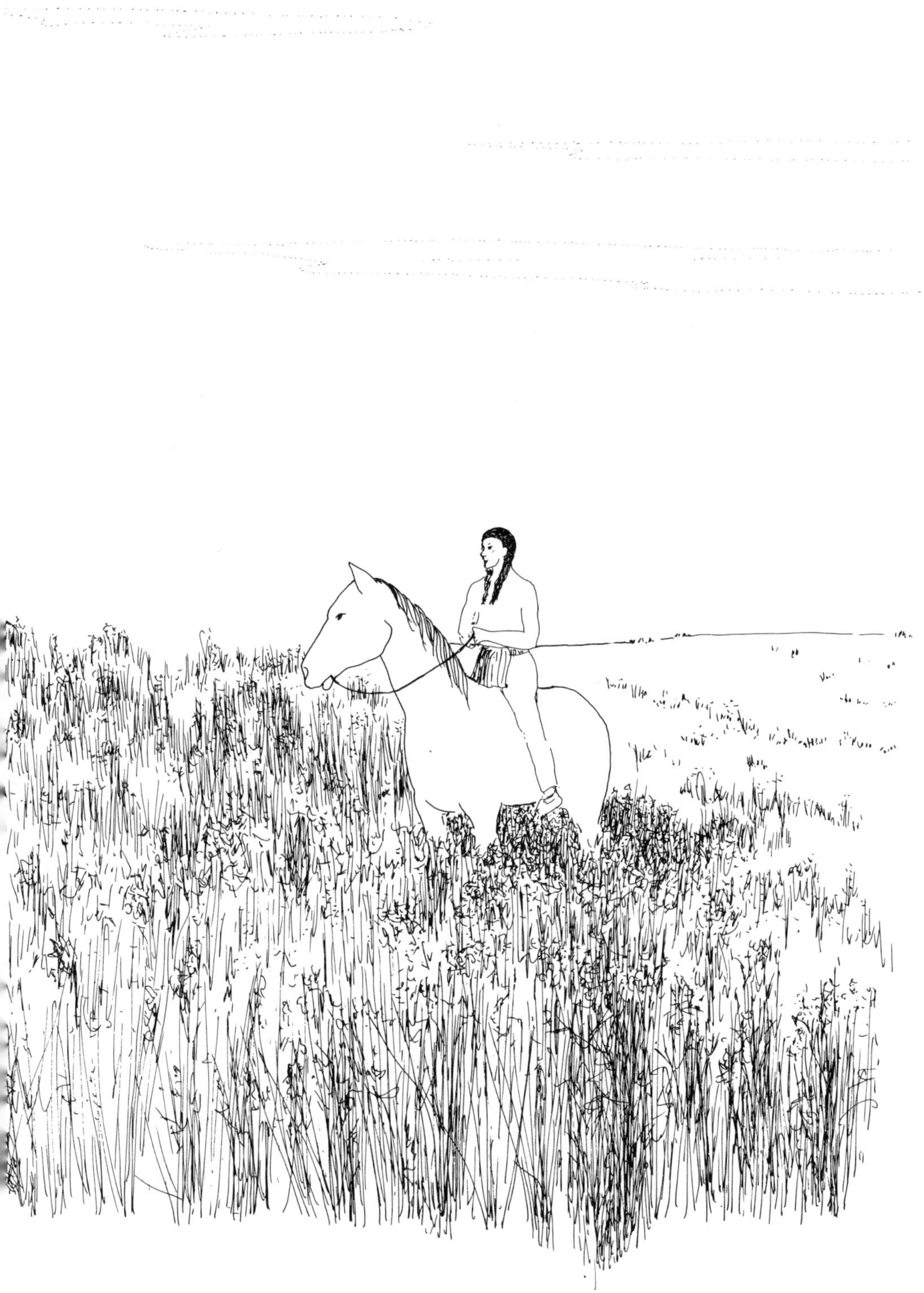

it again in a way he thought the Braves might understand, and as he continued they began to nod their heads in comprehension. Well, maybe some day he would be able to speak their language clearly, he thought. This was a beginning.

Wa'o'ka and Running Rabbit came towards the group with Running Rabbit still sitting on the mare's back. There were murmurs of surprise and approval from the Braves and Running Rabbit slipped off her back and brought her over to graze with the others. When they had eaten enough, the Braves led them back to the brush circle and there it was decided that not all the braves were needed to watch them all the time.

They would try it first with three Braves and Mi'ca, who was to watch especially for the wild one and keep him tethered when he was misbehaving. Each Brave would also choose his own special Sun'kawakan which he would try to sit on and ride with the help of the others. It would be better to work with one animal rather than keep changing. Dogs, after all, had one master and obeyed him. Those Braves who were not practicing riding should help the hunters on the Plains, since there were now many buffalo about.

Mi'ca found it wonderful to be working with the Sun'kawakan, and took great pleasure in coming in the early dawn every morning to release the Sun'kawakan from their brush enclosure. Each morning he would give his long low whistle, and Tangled Hoof would lift his head and whinny and come trotting towards Mi'ca so he would be the first to be taken down to the river. He would nuzzle Mi'ca's shoulder and Mi'ca would pat and stroke his long nose. Before Mi'ca could pull the brush enclosure closed, Tangled Hoof would give a small kick and would gallop to the river. Mi'ca gave a sigh. The other Sun'kawakan were always docile enough to let themselves be led to the river, but Tangled Hoof had too much spirit for that.

Black-eyed Susan
Hinyantan

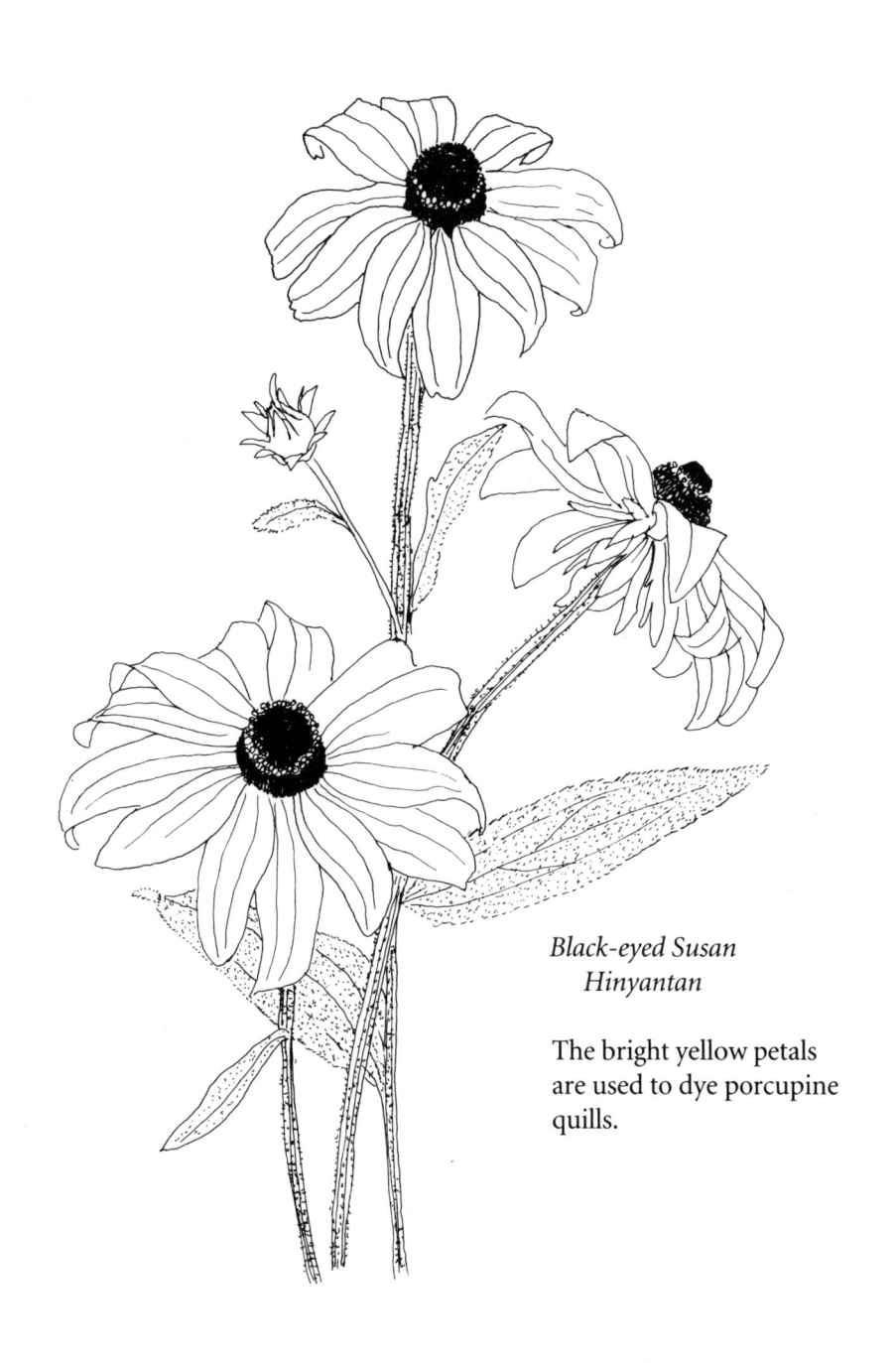

The bright yellow petals are used to dye porcupine quills.

Once in a while Mi'ca would hear the other boys of the camp. He watched them at their games from a distance. They ran races and tossed rings into the air and threw spears at them, and they practiced endlessly with their bows and arrows. Mi'ca envied their free time and longed to be practicing with them.

The tribe was a large one, many times the size of his own, and so there were many boys of his own age. But they ignored him as though he didn't exist, and, as a captive, he didn't. He was simply someone who was ordered to do certain tasks and if he performed badly, he would be treated badly. As far as the Tetons were concerned, he was not a young man destined to be a scout or a warrior or a healer. But Mi'ca liked working with the Sun'kawakan and so his duties were not a burden.

The Braves came early each morning to practice their riding. When they had begun to feel comfortable on their mounts, Mi'ca gathered up his courage and asked Wa'o'ka if he might now try to sit on Tangled Hoof's back. Wa'o'ka agreed, and Mi'ca mounted Tangled Hoof as gently as he could. But, when Mi'ca took the reins, Tangled Hoof suddenly ducked his head and kicked out his back legs. Then, with all four feet leaving the ground at nearly the same time he rose up into the air with an arched back. Then the feet came down together and he began bucking in circles. Mi'ca grabbed his mane as Tangled Hoof managed to twist his body into a crescent. Mi'ca went flying off Tangled Hoof's back and landed on the ground. None of the other Sun'kawakan had behaved quite like this! To see Mi'ca flying through the air made Wa'o'ka laugh. Mi'ca, when he had caught his breath, got up and laughed too. He caught hold of Tangled Hoof's reins and began to talk to him. This time he wasn't nice and comforting, but told Tangled Hoof in firm and slightly angry terms that he expected him to behave better!

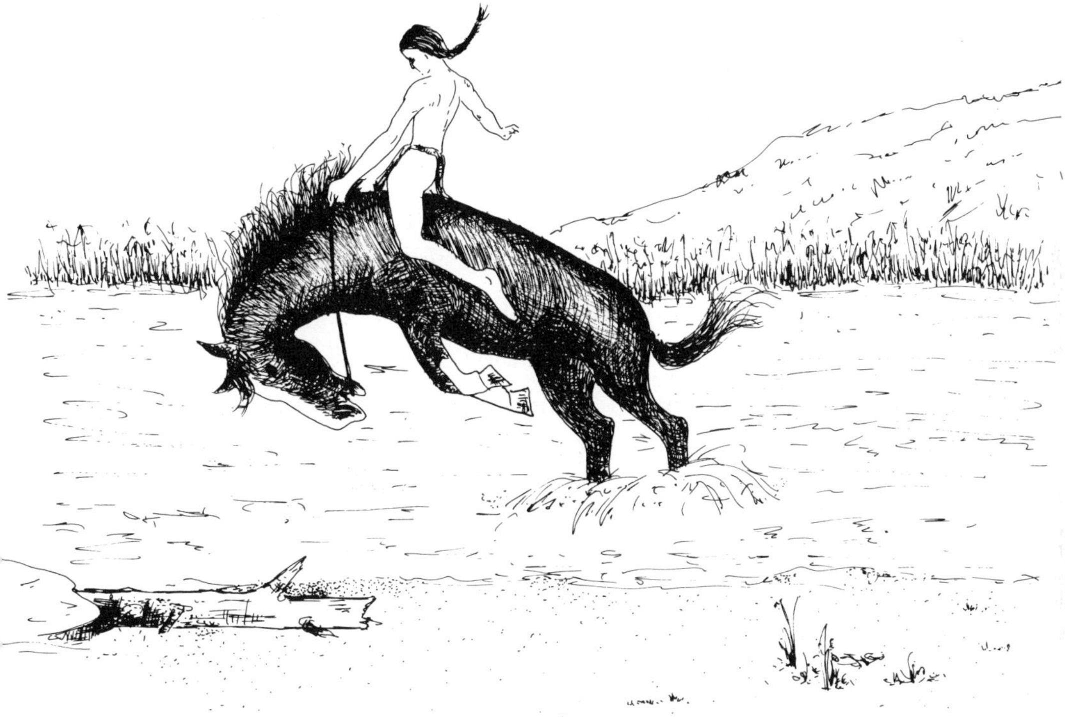

The next time it did go better. After a few kicks which weren't as bad as the first ones, Tangled Hoof gave a little shiver and stood still. Mi'ca patted his neck and talked into his ear and in a few minutes Tangled Hoof began to walk around the enclosure calmly. In his excitement at riding him, though, Mi'ca pressed his heels into the sides of the animal. Tangled Hoof immediately started galloping around the enclosure. Mi'ca was bouncing up and down on his back saying, "Heh, Ho, Ho!" but Tangled Hoof didn't listen, and instead gave a mighty leap and jumped over a low spot in the brush circle, throwing Mi'ca off just on the other side.

Tangled Hoof saw the other animals grazing some distance away and trotted over to them. He began grazing with them as though nothing had happened. Toka'la had seen the flying leap over the brush and the surprised look on Mi'ca's face when he had landed on the ground a second time. He laughed as hard as Wa'o'ka had to see Mi'ca sitting there.

Toka'la had an idea. "Let's take him down to the stream, so if you fall into the water it won't hurt so much. Maybe he can't buck as much then with the water swirling around his legs. Toka'la eased himself up on the back of one of the mares, and Mi'ca led Tangled Hoof down to the stream. Toka'la was right. Tangled Hoof tried hard to buck, but the water made it difficult for him and Mi'ca clung to him. After a while, he seemed to accept the idea that Mi'ca wasn't going to give up the idea of riding him.

As the Braves became more sure of themselves on their mounts, they also began to practice shooting with their bows as they rode. While the animals walked, this was no problem, but if they trotted or galloped it was very difficult to hit a target. It took much time and practice to shoot accurately and the Braves spent many weeks learning to do so while riding.

Dog
Sunka

Since most of Mi'ca's day was spent alone with the animals, he had to find things to do to keep up his skills. He first practiced throwing pebbles at objects, trying to be as accurate as Running Rabbit. He had been given back his knife and he fashioned sticks into spears, but he hadn't been given back his quiver with its bow and arrows. He missed these terribly since that meant he couldn't practice shooting. However, his relationship with Wa'o'ka was becoming closer, and Wa'o'ka began to treat him more like an uncle treats his sister's son. As there were no children yet in Wa'o'ka's tipi, Mi'ca became more of a family member than he otherwise might have been.

By day the camp was rather quiet except for the sounds of the children at play, but with the setting of the sun the Braves and Scouts who were back from the hunt began to shout invitations to their friends to come and eat with them and smoke a pipe together. At some tipis they got together to sing and dance while at others they gathered around the fire to hear stories about hunting or about war parties and brave deeds of the warriors. Everyone gathered around to hear the stories, old and young, women and children. But Mi'ca like it best when the tellers of the humorous stories came to Wa'o'ka's tipi. They were rarely found in their own lodges since they were so popular that everyone invited them to come and tell their tales.

When Wa'o'ka gave a feast he stepped outside his lodge and called out the names of those he wished to invite. The guests each brought their own bowls and spoons and greeted each other with great enthusiasm. The most important guest then sat closest to Wa'o'ka. When all were seated, his wife brought out the food and as it was passed around each guest threw a bit of meat into the fire to please the spirit of the fire. When they had finished eating, the

Tipi

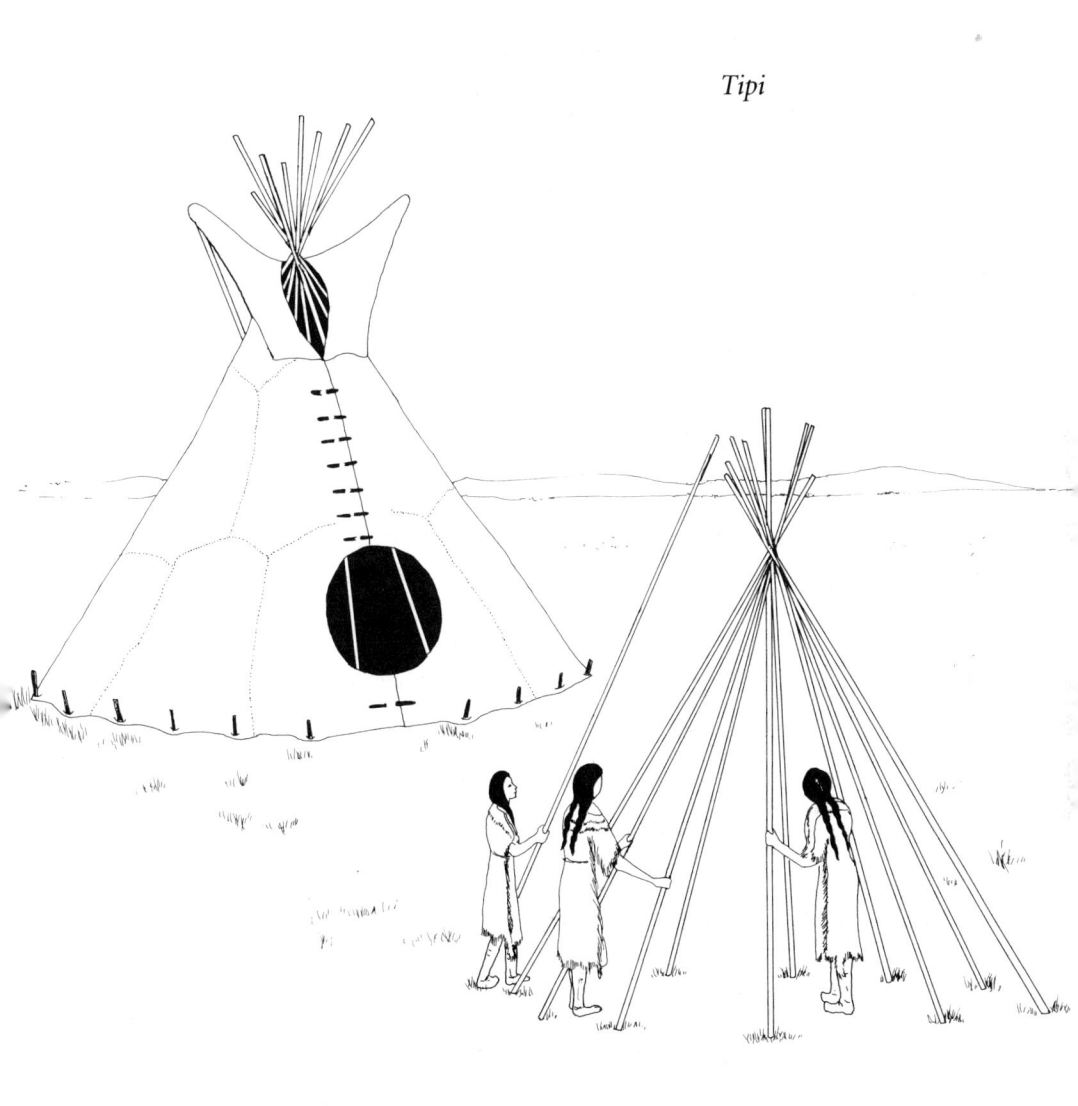

The poles of the Tipi are not set into the ground but the edges of the Tipi cover are pinned down with short pegs. The tipi can withstand the most violent storms. The top is left open for the smoke from the fire to escape. The opening is regulated by "smoke ears" which can be set according to which way the wind is blowing. The doorway always faces the rising sun pipe was lit and Wa'o'ka held it up and offered it to the sun and the sky and the earth below, and then after drawing a puff it was passed to the man at the end of the row and then from him to each man in turn, until it came back to the host. So it was smoked from East to West, imitating the daily course of the sun. After that the stories began and went on until Wa'o'ka taped the pipe and cried out, "Why, it's burned out!" That was the sign that the party was finished. Everyone rose quietly and left the tent without saying a word.

There were an enormous number of dogs in the camp. Wa'o'ka's tipi had nine. They slept outside and Wa'o'ka's wife threw them bones and scraps of meat. Mi'ca tried hard to make friends with them, but at first they were wary of him and bared their teeth if he came close. But gradually they became friendly and even allowed themselves to be petted. As the dogs became accustomed to Mi'ca they would let him cross the travois poles over their backs and lash on the harness. Although packing the travois was women's work, the men often helped in the making of the travois itself. Mi'ca wanted to understand exactly how the dog travois worked, because he had an idea that if one could make travois that the Sun'kawakan could pull, they would be able to carry much larger loads than any dog could. He was sure Tangled Hoof would be much too spirited and independent to ever be willing to drag the poles behind him, but there were two or three other Sun'kawakan who might be suitable. Mi'ca talked to Wa'o'ka about his idea, and Wa'o'ka said that he would think about it and talk to others.

The next morning Wa'o'ka took Mi'ca to visit Sitting Buffalo, known for his clever hands. He had been the most fearless hunter of the tribe and had killed more buffalo than any man, but one day when he had been out hunting, the herd swerved unexpectedly

Dog
Sunka

Puppy
Sunhpa'la

and a large buffalo cow with her calf trailing after her had charged at him and broken his leg. At the same time the buffalo cow had lost her balance and sat back on her haunches. Despite his wounds, the hunter drew his bow and killed the buffalo as she sat. Since that time he had been given the name of Sitting Buffalo. But his broken leg did not knit properly and he remained lame. Now that he was not able to hunt any more, he did many things around the camp.

When Mi'ca told him of his plans to make a travois for the Sun'kawakan, Sitting Buffalo thought about it and then told Mi'ca to go to the women and see if they had any old tipi poles. He finally found some and brought two long poles and together they fastened them crosswise at the top. Sitting Buffalo then bade Mi'ca to go and fetch the most even tempered animal and hold her bridle. When they got back, Sitting Buffalo then very slowly and gently lowered the poles onto her back. She shied a bit, but as they were lighter than a man she soon quieted, and Sitting Buffalo could experiment with different lengths and widths for a harness. He tried to fashion it in the same way as a dog harness, but it wasn't easy since the animal was so large.

As they worked, Toka'la, who turned out to be Sitting Buffalo's grandson, came to see what they were working on and with him was a large dog followed by a clumsy, wooly, excited little puppy. Toka'la greeted his grandfather deferentially and bade the dog to lie quietly. The puppy continued to bounce around.

"Ah, Toka'la, we are trying to make a giant sized travois. Please hold this strap while I tie the other one under his belly. Mi'ca, hold her bridle firmly, because she may not like to be tickled under the belly with all of my tying and retying of the knots," he said.

So, all three of them worked, patted, tied and retied until the strap seemed right. Then Toka'la said, "But we have forgotten the

Wolf
Sunkma'nitu tanka

cross piece at the back to hold the poles together!" He jumped up and went into the tipi to see if he could find some dog poles to make the cross pieces. After a bit he came back holding two old blackened poles and carrying more lengths of rawhide to tie them with. Mi'ca was glad Toka'la had been so enthusiastic in his help and glanced at him with a pleased smile. Toka'la caught his glance and smiled back.

After lashing the travois together, Sitting Buffalo asked the boys to walk slowly with her, one on each side of her head, to guide he as she dragged the light poles behind her. The animal took a few steps and then shied but with both boys holding her and talking to her she began to walk slowly forward down the path. Toka'la hadn't been working with the animals recently and the animal was wary of him and tended to pull towards Mi'ca,. But Toka'la was firm in his grasp. After they had walked near the tipi for a while, they turned and began to walk around the circle of tents and many women came crowding around to see what new and marvelous things the Sun'kawakan was capable of. They all began imagining things.

"They can pull bigger loads," one said. "And carry bigger tipis," added another. "They can haul more buffalo meat for us," added a third. The children said, "We can ride on top of the loads!"

Buffalo (Bison)
Tatan'ka

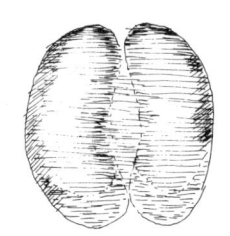

11
Buffalo

The next day Mi'ca went back to Sitting Buffalo and found Toka'la already there pulling leather strips back and forth through a knot hole to soften them. Mi'ca began to help him. It was tedious work and Sitting Buffalo said he would tell them about buffalo hunting while they worked.

"Our hunters often trick the buffalo into thinking that the hunters are something else than what they really are, for buffalo do not have very keen vision. The hunter puts a wolf skin on his back and pulls the wolf head over his own head. Then he creeps very slowly and carefully up to the herd. One or two wolves in broad daylight never disturb a herd unless there are small calves to be guarded. If the hunters find a group of buffalo grazing quietly they can creep in very close to them. Then ever so slowly and quietly they can raise up on one knee and let fly an arrow. If the arrow hits just under the ribs, the animal will drop to the ground without a sound. In this way perhaps two or three buffalo can be killed before the rest of the herd becomes alarmed and flees."

Mi'ca's deep brown eyes sparked with excitement. He could easily imagine himself as a hunter such as this, bringing down a shaggy buffalo. Toka'la then spoke up and said that he had once been with some other boys when they had found a buffalo calf hiding in the tall prairie grass. The herd had run off too fast for the

Creeping up on a Buffalo
herd with wolf skin disguise.

new little legs to keep up with them, and instinctively the calf had put his head down in the tall grass and kept very still. Toka'la had picked him up and slung him over his shoulders and then carried him back to the camp though the calf was heavy and kicked and struggled the whole way back.

Grandfather laughed and said he remembered how proud he was to see Toka'la with his first buffalo. "But now let us try this new harness on the mare. Pile buffalo hides on the travois and see if she will be willing to pull the heavy load."

Mi'ca and Toka'la were glad to stop work and help Sitting Buffalo with the travois. It worked quite well, and during the next few days they tried it with two other quiet animals. Everyone was pleased with their work and told them so. Wa'o'ka thought Mi'ca deserved a reward for his good thinking and hard work, so that evening when they were sitting before the fire in the tipi he called Mi'ca to stand before him. He very solemnly placed Mi'ca's quiver with its bow and arrows in his hands. Mi'ca's eyes danced with excitement and with a slight quaver in his voice asked if Wa'o'ka would teach him more about handling the weapon. Wa'o'ka was pleased by the request and sent Mi'ca to ask Toka'la to join them the following morning and they would go away from the camp and spend the day practicing.

Everything seemed more exciting to Mi'ca now that he had his bow and arrows. His days were filled with taking care of the Sun'kawakan, especially Tangled Hoof, and with helping the Braves while they practiced riding and shooting, and, of course, with being able to practice, himself. He was now becoming a good friend of Toka'la, and they often practiced shooting together. Sometimes they were with Wa'o'ka, and sometimes by themselves, and occasionally they practiced with a few of the other boys their age.

Goldenrod
Cannunga hu pteptecela

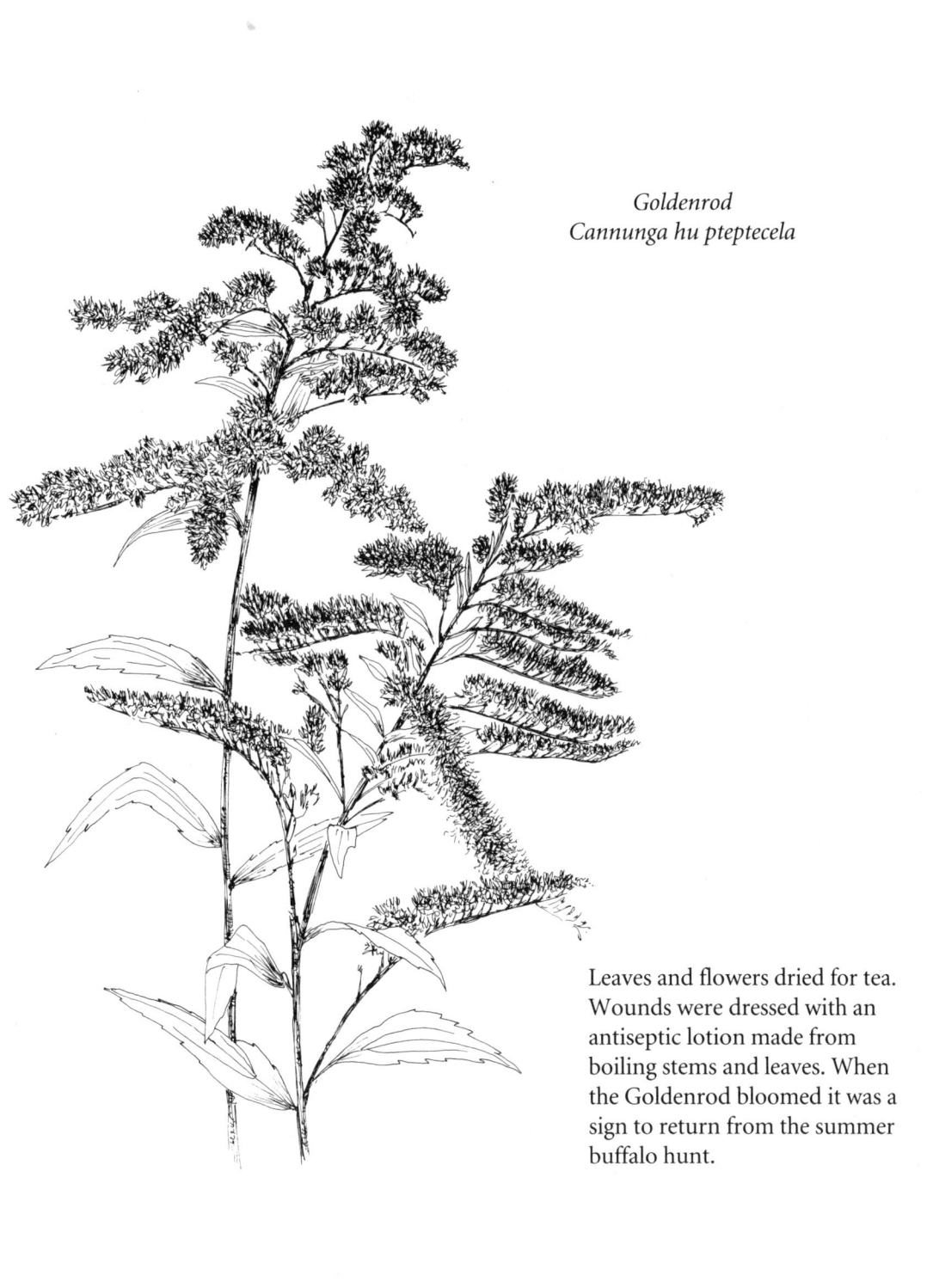

Leaves and flowers dried for tea. Wounds were dressed with an antiseptic lotion made from boiling stems and leaves. When the Goldenrod bloomed it was a sign to return from the summer buffalo hunt.

Then one day news passed from tipi to tipi that a large herd of buffalo was moving towards the cliff. Mi'ca ran to find Toka'la to ask him what was going on.

"Well," said Toka'la, "we set up our camp here by the stream each summer because it is close enough to the cliff, but far enough away so the noise and smoke of our campfires won't alarm the buffalo. Part of our band will try to drive a herd of buffalo over the cliff. There are large rocks placed in the shape of a V leading to the cliff. They were placed there long ago by our people and they form a funnel to lead the buffalo to the cliff.

"Many hunters move to the rear of the buffalo herd and creep up as close as possible. Only one hunter, the 'Buffalo Caller,' goes to the front of the herd, and he is the bravest of all. The buffalo are always ready to run if they see the lead cow run, so the buffalo caller puts a buffalo head over his head and acts like a lead cow. He pretends to graze, and then moves slowly towards the cliff. When the exact moment comes, he runs toward the cliff. Then the hunters at the rear rise up and wave their robes to frighten the herd so that they will run forward. When the buffalo see which way the lead cow goes, they will all begin to stampede towards the cliff. As they run, those of us who have been hiding behind the rocks have to jump up and yell and shout and wave our buffalo robes to keep them going in the right direction. When they get to the cliff the buffalo caller must throw off his disguise and run behind a large stone near the edge of the cliff so he won't get trampled to death. The buffalo will not be able to swerve in time and will tumble over the cliff.

"Come on! Now we must run to the Council Tipi to see who will be chosen to go. Most of the people will stay here, but I hope we can go!"

Buffalo Fall
Wanaunka

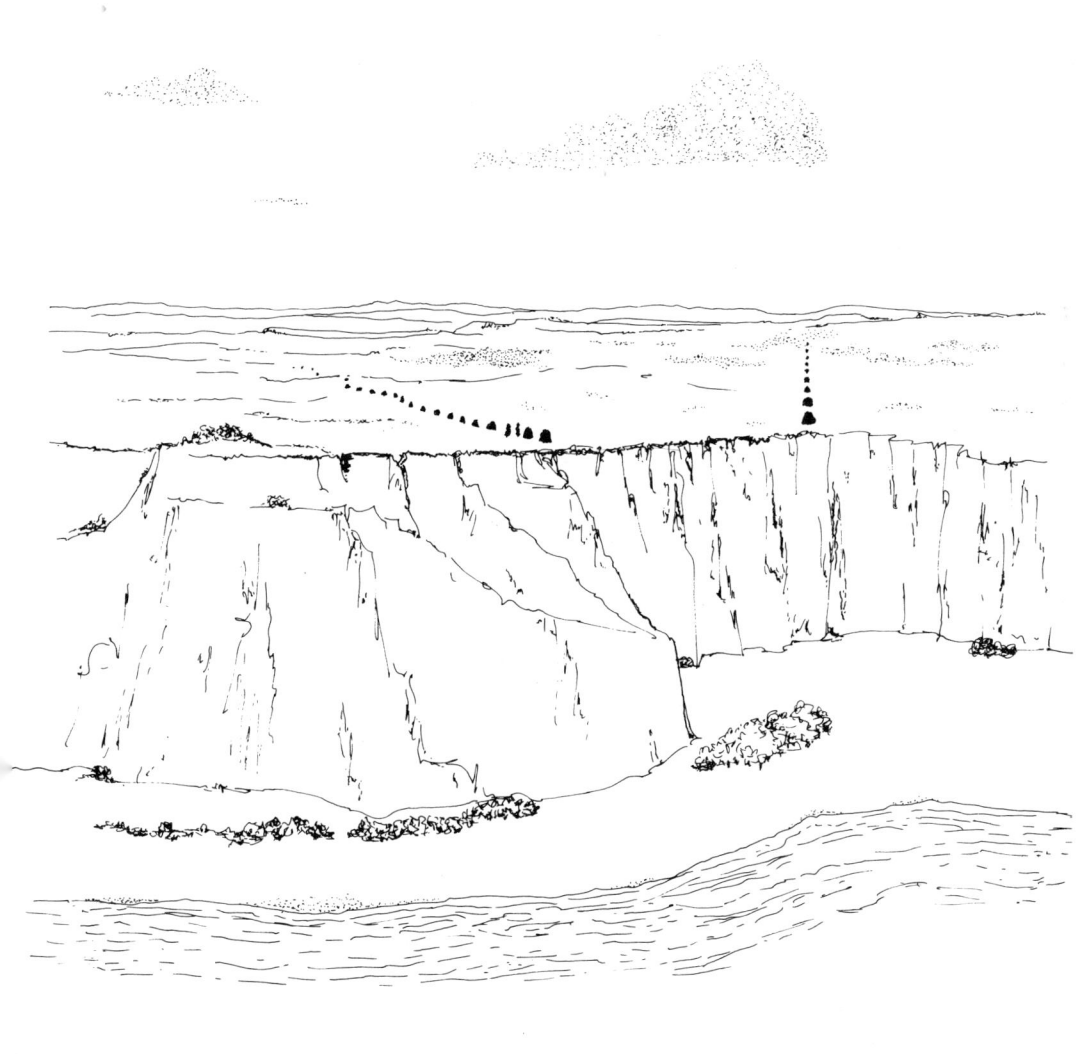

Names were called out by the Chief. Wa'o'ka and Lark Woman would go and help, and Mi'ca as part of that family would also go. Toka'la and his family and his grandfather were also chosen. They were to try loading the travois on the backs of the Sun'kawakan. When all the people had been chosen there was much laughter and excitement, but no one in the camp seemed to be hurrying, for everyone moved so quietly. Everyone seemed to know his or her work and they did it easily and quickly.

It made a big group moving out across the prairie. After two days travel they camped in the river valley below the cliff, and it was just in time. That night the camp crier went around crying, "Heya, heya, ha-a-a-a! Hunters, listen to me! Tomorrow morning if all goes well, White Eagle will lead the buffalo to the cliff and will bring buffalo meat tumbling down for our people. The hunters are all to sing the song of the coyote, the greatest hunter of them all, before we sleep tonight!"

Mi'ca and the others watched White Eagle get out his paint bag and rub reddish-brown ocher on his face and hands. The drum began to beat and White Eagle sat down and began to sing the coyote song. He lit his Peace Pipe, then held the mouthpiece first to the Father Sky and to Mother Earth and to the four winds, the West, North, East, and South. White Eagle sang "He-yó, Sun which is powerful, He-yó, Old Man! Give us food tomorrow and give me power to bring great quantities of food to my people." He then passed the pipe around the circle from left to right. All the people joined in the refrain to call the spirits of the buffalo and charm them into a happy departure to the spirit land.

The next morning when the sun rose, White Eagle stepped from his tipi and tossed a feather into the air to see which way the wind was blowing. The air was quiet with only a light breeze from

*Buffalo Fall
Wanaunka*

the west. That was good, for the scent of the people would not be carried to the buffalo.

At his signal all the people climbed to the top of the cliff above their camping place. Then Mi'ca saw the ever widening rows of rocks that extended out onto the plain in an enormous V shape. Far back, the buffalo were quietly feeding. White Eagle first sent some of the braves to circle around to the far side of the buffalo herd, ready to stampede the herd when the time came. They circled wide and moved so slowly and carefully in the prairie grass that even the people waiting could not see them. While they waited, White Eagle motioned to the rest of the people to move carefully towards the buffalo and hide themselves behind the rocks. He put the buffalo head on like a huge hat, and draped the robe over his back.

After all the people were in place, he moved to where the buffalo could see him, but well within the V of the rocks. He stood still and pawed the sun-yellowed grass with his foot and swayed his head from side to side. One buffalo cow became curious and began to walk towards him. White Eagle bent over as though he were eating grass, and then walked a short distance towards the cliff. Soon the other cows began to follow. White Eagle stopped and pretended to eat again and the herd again became quiet, but they had begun to move inside the V. Mi'ca could see Toka'la peering out from a rock on the other side.

White Eagle then began to bleat like a wounded buffalo calf. Some of the nearest buffalo stopped feeding and moved toward him. Then all the men on the far side of the herd leaped into the air, yelling and waving their robes, and the buffalo stampeded away from them. The lead buffalos followed White Eagle who was now running towards the cliff. Soon the whole herd was running.

Sunflowers

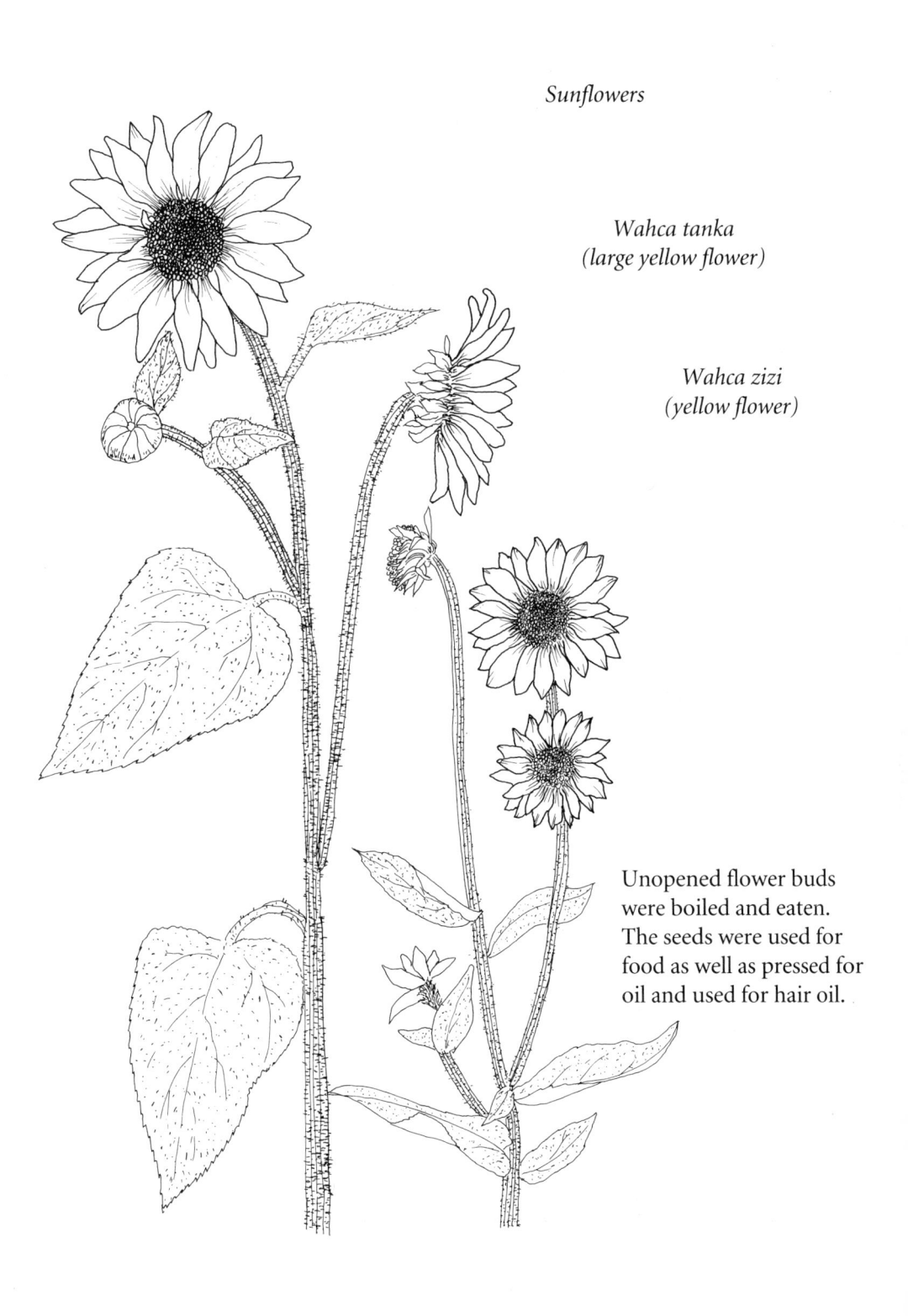

Wahca tanka
(large yellow flower)

Wahca zizi
(yellow flower)

Unopened flower buds were boiled and eaten. The seeds were used for food as well as pressed for oil and used for hair oil.

At that moment a Brave sitting on a high rise stood up. That was the sign to those behind the rocks to stand and wave their robes and soon everyone was waving and yelling. When the buffalo began to run they lowered their heads to bring their near-sighted eyes closer to the ground. Their horns glistened in the sunlight as their hooves turned the dust into a brown swirling mass, and their snorts and cries drowned out the voices of the Tetons. White Eagle dashed behind the last rock before the drop, breathless but safe.

Mi'ca flapped his robe and yelled at the stampeding mass. The ground under his feet shook with the rhythmic pounding of the hooves of the buffalo. After only a few minutes of noise and dust and a glimpse of the wild terror in the buffalo's eyes, the herd had charged past Mi'ca and raced on towards the cliff. Mi'ca and the others ran after herd to keep them from turning around and running off towards the plain. The dust was thick and brown and the people were coughing as much as yelling. As the first buffalos fell over the cliff, the ones behind tried to stop and turn back, but many were forced over the cliff by the charging mass behind them. But eventually most of the herd was able to turn and escape. The people waving the robes had to be very careful not to be trampled by the frightened buffalo as they turned to get out of the trap. As soon as the noise died down and the dust began to settle, Mi'ca and Toka'la ran to look over the cliff.

There was such a pile of buffalo and so many people that it was hard to see what was going on. When they reached the bottom of the cliff they found everyone busily removing hides and cutting meat into long strips. Lark Woman was already placing a hide on the ground and piling the meat on it. She called to Mi'ca and Toka'la to bring three Sun'kawakan. When they returned with the Sun'kawakan they found that a fire had been made and everyone

Buffalo Dance

had stopped work to eat. Some were eating raw meat and others were broiling pieces of meat over the fire. Lark Woman had broiled some pieces of liver on a stick for them. "Liver is the first meat the hunters eat, so eat now, and feel the strength of the buffalo come into your arms," she said. Both were careful to throw small pieces of meat into the fire to give thanks to the buffalo spirit.

When they had finished eating, Lark Woman helped them load the travois and she and the two boys led the animals back to the campsite where Grandfather helped unload them. The two boys then took the animals back to the cliff while Lark Woman stayed at the campsite and began to cut the meat in long thin strips and hang it on poles to dry in the sunshine. Mi'ca and Toka'la were able to bring the animals back and forth many times. The people at the cliff were very pleased. "Now we won't have to bring our dogs to the cliff to haul our meat," several said. Wa'o'ka explained to Mi'ca that the dogs love to eat the meat themselves and often quarreled over it and when they had stuffed themselves they preferred to lie down and sleep rather than drag heavy loads.

When the sun was low in the sky the cry went up to halt the work. They gathered wood and brush and built several large bonfires to frighten off the wolves and coyotes. Sentries were chosen to tend the fires all night. The rest of the people walked back to the campsite.

When everyone had returned, the hunters formed a circle to give thanks to Wakan-Tanka for giving them good hunting and to honor the spirits of the buffalo. They set the buffalo heads on their heads and some hunters held gourd rattles. White Eagle raised his face to the sky and began to chant, and the hunters began shouting "Oo-oo-oo-oo!" swaying their heads from side to side and pawing the ground. They began to dance very slowly and then faster and

Wolf
Sunkma'nitu tanka

Wolf
Sungma'nitu tanka

faster. Mi'ca had never before seen a Buffalo Dance. He became so excited that he jumped up and began to dance behind Wa'o'ka and tried to follow his steps, but he couldn't follow the words of the chant. In a few moments everyone was dancing, and the men in the center got wilder and wilder, stamping and pawing like buffalo. The women danced in a circle around the outside, using a slower, shuffling motion. The dancing went on until everyone was quite exhausted and the sky was dark. Only then did the dance end and everyone went to bed. Mi'ca couldn't fall asleep right away. He could hear the wolves howling and the Sun'kawan stirring restlessly nearby. He kept thinking of the buffalo, and he knew he had never felt so happy.

Mi'ca and Toka'la spent the next day leading the Sun'kawakan back and forth from cliff to camp. Boys came from the village bringing many dogs dragging travois, but they did not take them as far as the cliff, only as far as the campsite where they were loaded with the dried meat to carry back to the village. They had brought some of the biggest dogs. Mi'ca thought they looked almost like wolves themselves and they were very strong. Toka'la was delighted to see his dog among them, but the puppy had been left behind. That night the wolves howled, and the camp was filled with the noises of the dogs howling in response. "Listen to that racket!" the people said, "They are talking to their brothers out there on the prairie!"

The next morning the dog packs were loaded and the dogs dragged them back to the village. On the third day when the boys got back to the cliff, there were paw prints very close to the buffalo. Wolves and coyotes had been circling the kill and had become more and more bold in defying the guards and their fires. Toka'la and Mi'ca made a game of trying to count how many prints of

Travois
Sunonkonpa

each animal they could find and then guess how many animals had been there in the night.

One man, named Bone Cracker, sat off to one side with a huge pile of bones. As soon as the others had finished removing the meat from the large bones, they tossed them on his pile. He pushed the big leg bones into the hot ashes of the night sentry fires which made them easy to crack and get the marrow out. His wife then carefully stuffed the marrow into skin bags, as everyone needed marrow to mix with the powdered dried meat to make pemmican. When they brought the marrow back to the tipi village it would be divided among all the people the same way the meat was divided.

Another man was gathering up the best horns and bones to be used to make tools; hide scrapers, horn spoons,or, spongy bones to be used as paint brushes on the hides. They would be piled up in the village until winter when everyone had more time to make things from them.

Each morning the dogs with their travois were brought from the village to carry back the meat and hides. Mi'ca was surprised at how completely every buffalo was used. Even though many buffalo had been killed, nothing was wasted. When they finally broke camp and went back to the main village, about all that was left to be shared by the wolves and coyotes and hawks and eagles were the lungs and the cracked bones. It had been an extraordinarily good hunt and everyone was laughing and singing all the way back.

Buffalo (Bison)
Tatan'ka

Sign for buffalo

12

Swift Arrow

All the Sun'kawakan were behaving well even when the Braves were shooting from their backs. The Braves could now go in groups of four or five, all of them racing their animals and shooting at the same time. They were waiting impatiently for the day that more buffalo would be found so they could ride out and try chasing them down from on top of their Sun'kawakan.

One day, in the Moon-of-the-Red-Cherries, a Scout came running into the camp. Buffalo had been sighted not far off. The Braves, he said, should get on their Sun'kawakan, and ride out to see if they could get close enough to bring down a few.

The Braves ran to get their bows and arrows, as did Mi'ca. All of the Braves leaped onto their mounts and started to ride off. Toka'la was riding the mare. He waved to Mi'ca and rode off with the others. No one had indicated Mi'ca could not go, so he rushed to the brush corral. As he eased himself on to Tangled Hoof he whispered into his ear to please, please, behave today and make his first buffalo hunt turn out to be the greatest thing which had ever happened to him. Tangled Hoof had his own idea of how to do things, so he first galloped around the brush enclosure before he gave a leap forward and moved out onto the prairie. The other hunters had gotten far ahead by now.

Mi'ca strained his eyes to see the herd, but all he saw were the

Prairie Dog
Pispiza

riders ahead of him. He had never been allowed to go very far out on the plains west of the camp, so he was rather surprised to see that they were covered with hundreds of little mounds. This was a prairie dog town and every mound was alive with inhabitants. The prairie dogs sat upon their haunches with their tiny paws held to their chests. Mi'ca laughed and waved to them. They looked so much like tiny people, and many tales said that they had once been real people. But when the prairie dogs felt the earth tremble from Tangled Hoof's pounding hooves they all popped down into their holes and disappeared.

Mi'ca had ridden Tangled Hoof many times after that first bucking start and he had learned to shoot from his back, but this was the first time the two had been out for a really long run. It was an exhilarating feeling; pleasantly scary and absolutely marvelous. Tangled Hoof galloped with long clean strides. Mi'ca felt like an arrow shot from a bow, so swiftly were they moving along. The wind in his face made his long black braids fly out behind. Mi'ca marveled at how smoothly Tangled Hoof's powerful muscles carried them across the open plains.

Finally he saw the herd of buffalo in a small group far off to the left. He saw the riders slow to a walk so that they could come near the herd without alarming them. As Mi'ca came closer he pulled out his bow and strung it and drew an arrow out of his quiver.

All of a sudden, the riders kicked their mounts and gave chase to a group of buffalo who were slightly apart from the others. The Sun'kawakan ran like the wind and gained on the buffalo until they were running alongside them. The Braves let fly their arrows and several buffalo dropped. Mi'ca raced Tangled Hoof to join in.

The dust was rising but he could see the herd swerve to the right and the riders aiming straight ahead towards them. Again the

arrows flew and two more buffalo fell. A third buffalo swerved and Wa'o'ka turned his animal to the right to avoid his path. Mi'ca dug his heels into Tangled Hoof to bring him closer to the others. At the same moment a huge bull spotted Wa'o'ka and charged towards him. Wa'o'ka let fly an arrow which missed its mark and to Mi'ca's horror he saw Wa'o'ka's mount step into a prairie dog's hole and stumble. Wa'o'ka was thrown to the ground right in the path of the charging bull. Mi'ca's bow was ready and he shot with all his might, aiming at the spot just under the ribs. The bull gave a terrible snort and fell pawing to the ground just inches from Wa'o'ka.

Mi'ca slid from Tangled Hoof and dropped the reins. Tangled Hoof stood shivering from the wild race and Wa'o'ka slowly sat up. He wasn't hurt, just bruised. His mount was a little way off, limping, but apparently not seriously injured.

"Aieee, brave one, you saved my life!" Wa'o'ka exclaimed. "Let's rest a bit until the others turn and come back. I don't think either I or my mount can continue the chase today. That was a close call! I owe you my life, and I thank you with all my heart. But Ho! It was exciting, wasn't it? Think of riding as fast as a buffalo can run; faster, really! Aieee-ee, it was a good chase!"

Mi'ca crouched beside Wa'o'ka and placed his quiver on the ground. Only then did he finally realize that he had used his special arrow, and had killed his first buffalo. And, not just any buffalo, this was an enormous bull. He thought back to his Vision and gave a start of recognition. "Ho!" Mi'ca cried as he jumped up to pull his arrow out of the bull. "You are my Vision animal!"

The other Braves circled back and were amazed when they saw how many buffalo had fallen. But, when they reached Wa'o'ka and Mi'ca and saw them sitting on the ground beside the enormous bull they jumped off their animals and crowded around to hear what had happened. Wa'o'ka told Mi'ca to stand and tell the whole story, especially the part about the Vision-quest. The Braves were full of praise for Mi'ca. Toka'la suddenly shouted, "Let's eat some liver from this animal to celebrate and give thanks. We can build a fire right here." Nothing had ever tasted so good to Mi'ca.

The Braves helped Mi'ca to remove the hide, for the buffalo was much too heavy for Mi'ca to roll over by himself. They scraped the hide and handed it to Mi'ca. They would send the dog travois to carry back all the meat they had brought down. Wa'o'ka's mount couldn't be ridden with his sore leg, so Toka'la led him behind his mare. But Wa'o'ka needed a ride back to camp. Tangled Hoof was by far the biggest of the Sun'kawakan, but the question was whether he would let two people sit on his back. Mi'ca got on and then Wa'o'ka slowly and gently mounted behind him. Tangled Hoof got excited, and Mi'ca had to struggle a bit with him, but he soon calmed down. Mi'ca urged him forward and it was as though he had done this many times. A murmur of surprise went through the Braves; Tangled Hoof was becoming part of the tribe! Everyone was pleased. Mi'ca had tamed Tangled Hoof and he had saved the life of one of their best braves. They smiled with their eyes and called words of praise to him as they rode back towards the camp.

That night in camp the Chief called everyone together before the Council Fire. Again all the Braves and Scouts and Hunters sat close to the Chief and the women and children formed the outer circle. Mi'ca hung back. He didn't know quite where he was supposed to be. He was still their captive. The Chief called the Braves to tell what marvelous things had happened today because of the Sun'kawakan. Many Braves told the story of the hunt.

When it was Wa'o'ka's turn he told how Mi'ca had shot his arrow and killed the enraged bull and saved his life. The crowd murmured its surprise and pleasure at the story. The Chief then called to Mi'ca to step forward with his bow and arrows.

Mi'ca moved through the crowd until he stood before the Chief. The Chief pointed to the ground and there stood a new pair of moccasins made in the style of the Teton. Mi'ca was stunned. He knew if he discarded his old moccasins and put on the new ones that he would no longer be a captive, but a new Brave in the Teton tribe. It was such an honor that he gasped -forgetting for a moment to look serious and unsmiling. It took him only a moment to decide. Yes! He loved his life here on the prairie with Tangled Hoof and buffalos and his friends Toka'la and Wa'o'ka. He stepped out of his old moccasins with the holes worn through the soles. He thought of how hard his sister had worked on them. Then he thought of his mother and wished she was here to share his pride. He bent down and slipped on the new moccasins and stood proudly before the Chief.

The Chief put his hand on Mi'ca's shoulder and said, "Truly you are worthy of becoming a member of our great Teton tribe by your brave deeds today, as well as by your exceptionally good nature which we have observed over the time you have been living with us. We must have a great feast to celebrate your becoming one of our Braves. You will no longer have the name of a child, Mi'ca, Coyote Cub. From this day on you shall have a Brave's name. You shall be called Swift Arrow."

Mi'ca stood tall and looked at all the people crowding around him and smiling at him. He was one of them now, and they were proud of him. He began to speak. "Many moons ago when I lived among the tribe of the Wahpeton, my Grandfather helped me to fashion this bow and arrow. It was the beginning of my instruction to become a Brave. When the bow and arrow were finished we

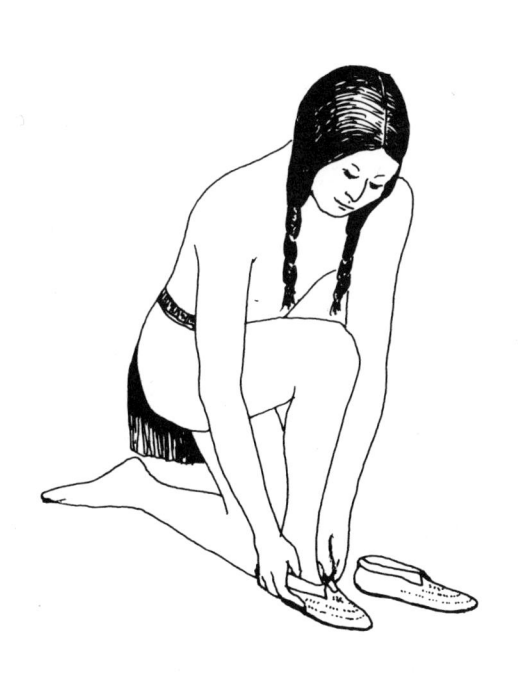

carried them to the tipi of Wapi'ya, our wise medicine man, for his blessing. Wapi'ya was much moved by the silvery arrow which I now hold, and said that it truly contained powerful medicine of an unknown sort. He told me then that my future was surely bound up with this silvery arrow and that it was destined to change my life in some mysterious way that was hidden from him. The power of the arrow has been revealed today and I am proud to become a Brave of the Teton, and proud to receive the name of Swift Arrow."

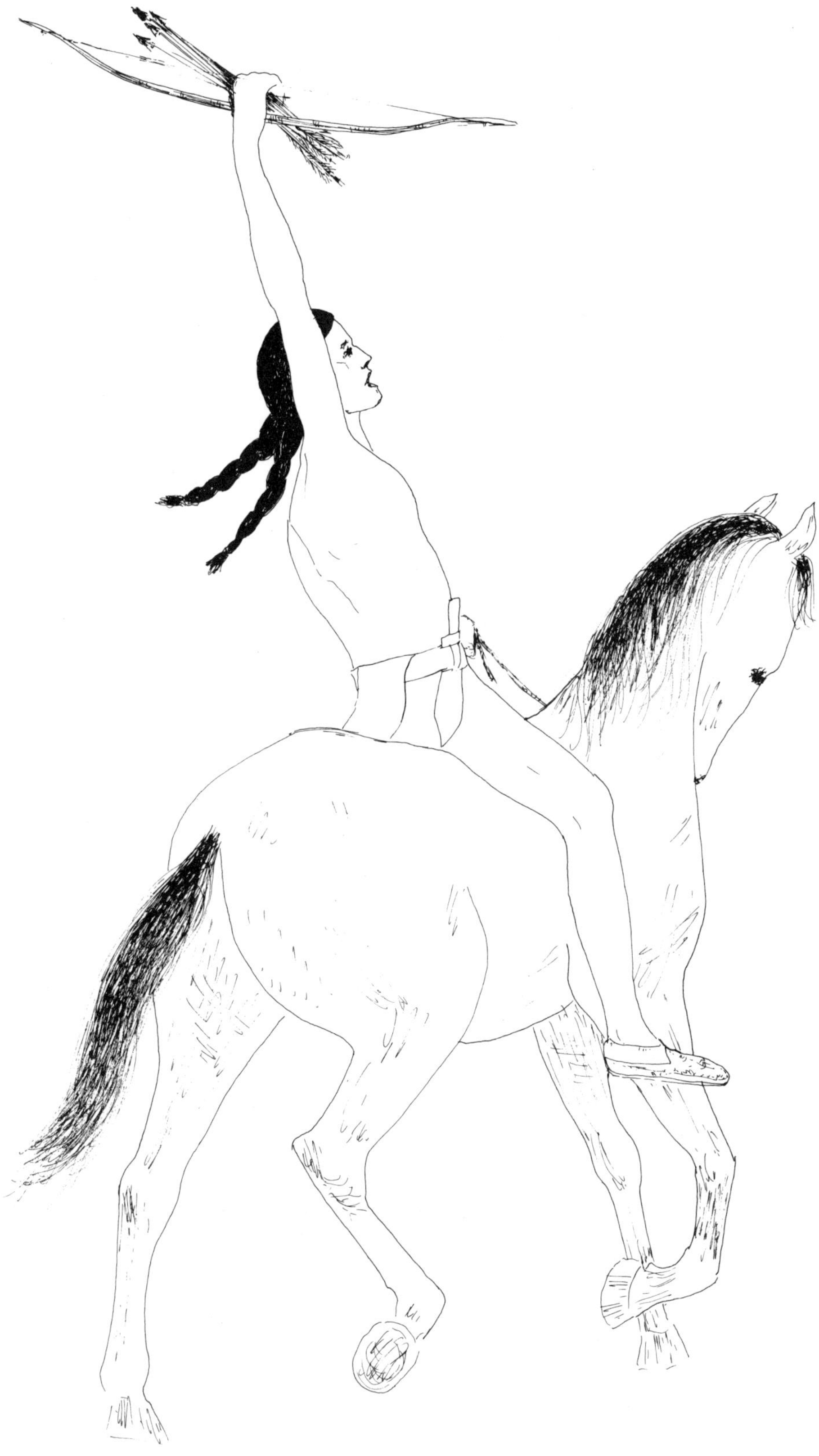